The
Punishment

The
Punishment

TAHAR BEN JELLOUN

TRANSLATED FROM THE FRENCH BY

LINDA COVERDALE

YALE UNIVERSITY PRESS ■ NEW HAVEN & LONDON

A MARGELLOS
WORLD REPUBLIC OF LETTERS BOOK

The Margellos World Republic of Letters is dedicated to making literary works from around the globe available in English through translation. It brings to the English-speaking world the work of leading poets, novelists, essayists, philosophers, and playwrights from Europe, Latin America, Africa, Asia, and the Middle East to stimulate international discourse and creative exchange.

Yale University Press books may be purchased in quantity for educational, business, or promotional use. For information, please e-mail sales.press@yale.edu (U.S. office) or sales@yaleup.co.uk (U.K. office).

Set in Electra and Nobel types by Tseng Information Systems, Inc.
Printed in the United States of America.

Library of Congress Control Number: 2019948754
ISBN 978-0-300-24302-4 (hardcover : alk. paper)

A catalogue record for this book is available from the British Library.

This paper meets the requirements of ANSI/NISO Z39.48-1992 (Permanence of Paper).

10 9 8 7 6 5 4 3 2 1

CONTENTS

"You go into great detail, is this book autobiographical?"

"Completely, I invented nothing. It is an account, not a novel. My memory was extraordinarily faithful and brought back to me everything that happened."

Tahar Ben Jelloun
Interview, February 13, 2018
www.yabiladi.com

The
Punishment

July 16, 1966, is one of those mornings that my mother has tucked away in a corner of her memory, she says, so she can remember to tell her gravedigger all about it. A gloomy morning with a white and pitiless sky.

Many words have gone missing from that day. What remains are vacant, downcast eyes. Dirty hands snatch a son not yet twenty years old from his mother. Commands and insults fly: "We'll teach him what's what, this sonofabitch!" The army jeep spits nauseating fumes. My mother fears the worst, tries desperately not to collapse. It's a time when young men are disappearing, when frightened people keep their voices low, suspecting the walls of recording thoughts voiced against the regime, the king, and his henchmen, those ruthless soldiers and undercover policemen whose cruelty hides behind hollow phrases. Before leaving, one of the two men tells my father, "Tomorrow your kid must report to the camp at El Hajeb, general's orders. Here's the train ticket, third class. He'd better not run away."

The jeep belches one last blast of exhaust and takes off, tires screeching. I knew that I was on the list. They'd gone to Moncef's house the day before, and he'd warned me that we were in for it. Someone had told him beforehand, apparently, perhaps his father, who has a cousin at army headquarters. On an old map of Morocco, I look for El Hajeb. "It's next to Meknès," my father says. "It's a village where there are only soldiers."

The next morning, I'm on the train with my older brother. He has insisted on going all the way there with me. We have no specific information. Just that curt summons.

▪

My crime? To have participated on March 23, 1965, in a peaceful student demonstration that was bloodily repressed. I was with a friend when suddenly, right in front of us, members of the Chabakoni brigade, as they're called—*ça va cogner,* "gonna get rough"—began savagely beating the demonstrators for no reason at all. Frantic with fear, we ran and ran until we finally found shelter in a mosque. Along the way, I saw bodies lying on the ground in their own blood. Later I saw mothers rushing to hospitals in search of their children. I saw panic, and hatred. Above all, I saw the face of a monarchy that had given soldiers free rein to restore order by any means whatever. On that day, the division between the people and their army was sealed. There were rumors in town that General Oufkir in person had fired on crowds in Rabat and Casablanca from a helicopter.

That same evening, the Union Nationale des Étudiants Marocains (UNEM) held a secret meeting in the kitchen of the university cafeteria, a gathering I was naive enough to attend. Even before it was over we heard the jeeps arrive: we had clearly been betrayed. The union leaders had long thought that someone was tipping off the police and suspected one guy in particular, a thin, ugly, and very smart little fellow, but they could never prove anything against him. The police came in, rounded up the older students, and took down the names of all the others. I thought I'd simply had a close call . . .

■

The seats are wooden, the train cars date from before World War II, and we creep along like a snail. The landscapes drift by with a strange indolence. From time to time, the train stops. We look out the windows and breathe in air polluted by the locomotive's smokestack. People clamber aboard laden with baskets, sacks, even live roosters. They smoke foul tobacco. I cough and turn away. I think about the meetings we held over the past few months: useless, unproductive. At our age, it's normal for us to want to change things, and we aren't doing anything wrong. We talk for hours, discussing the hard facts of the situation. We want to fight against injustice, repression, the lack of freedom. What could be more noble? Most of us don't belong to any political party. One of us is a Communist, it's true, or at least he's always championing communism, but we don't try to find out what that really means for him. He hates America. Me, I adore jazz and American movies, so I don't understand his stubborn attitude. He thinks everything that comes from the United States is bad, harmful, untouchable. He doesn't drink Coca-Cola, for example. That's his way of expressing his anti-Americanism. Well, a little glass of Coke, I like it, especially in the summer. That's hardly enough to make me feel complicit in the atrocities committed by GIs in Vietnam.

The train gently gets going again. My brother has dozed off. The peasant with the roosters stinks. I even think I see a louse or a flea on the dingy collar of his old shirt. He takes out a long pipe, packs it with what looks like tobacco, and lights up. It's kif.[1] He smokes quietly without even wondering if it might bother us. I feel a migraine coming on. I'm prepared for this: when I get an aspirin from my bag, the peasant holds out a bottle of water, and I wish I'd brought a glass along too. I thank him and swallow the tablet. I stand up and walk a little way along the aisle. In the distance I can see a shepherd taking a nap under a tree. I envy him. I tell myself he has no idea how lucky he is. There's no one to punish him, and I know he hasn't done anything, but personally I'm innocent as well and here I am on this miserable train headed for a barracks where I have no idea what's going to happen to me! I see a peasant woman go by and think of my fiancée. That hurts. Zayna didn't come to say good-bye to me before I left. And I'd even called her. Her mother had answered the phone coldly. When I told Zayna what was happening to me, she didn't say anything, or rather she sighed, as if I were annoying her. "Goodbye," she told me, and hung up. I'm in love with her, I think constantly about when we met, in the French Library. Our hands had reached for the same book, *The Stranger* by Camus. "I have to write a report about it," she told me, and I'd quickly replied, "I could help you, I've already studied it." That's how we came to meet several afternoons at the Café Pino, rue de Fez. We talked a long time about this story of an Arab murdered because of the sun, or sorrow. "His mother dies," she'd say to me, "and he doesn't know exactly when? He's an unworthy son ..." I too didn't understand how a son could not be sure about which day his mother died. After all this astonishment, we looked at each other like Cary Grant and Ingrid Bergman. I often accompanied her all the way home. One evening, taking advantage of a power outage, I stole a kiss. She clung to me, and it was the beginning of a love story in which everything seemed momentous. We had to hide to love each other. She preserved her virginity and I made do with caressing her. Darkness was our accomplice. There was an excitement about these furtive embraces that left us trembling. Rich in feverish uncertainties, our love intoxicated us. Impossible to forget, those moments that played out later in our dreams. The next day, we'd tell each other about our night. We were giddy and happy. To all that, His Majesty's police were about to put a brutal and definitive end.

◾

The train enters the station in Meknès at around seven that evening. Torrid heat. The last bus between Meknès and El Hajeb left a half hour earlier. Spending the night in this unfamiliar city is a discouraging prospect. My brother finds an inexpensive little hotel. The guy at the reception desk is blind in one eye, hasn't shaved for a few days, and spits on the floor with a sharp little sound, it's a tic. He makes us pay in advance and hands over a large key, saying, "No whores allowed." I look down, embarrassed in front of my big brother. A room with two beds. Dirty sheets. Randomly stained with blood. We look at each other without a word. No choice. If you're poor, you can't be fastidious about soiled sheets. My brother produces a roast chicken from his bag: our mother has thought of everything. A big loaf of bread, some Laughing Cow cheese, and two oranges. Sitting right on the floor, we eat without comment. Looking to wash our hands, we realize that there is neither sink nor toilet in the room. Everything is out in the hall and repulsively foul. We stare at one another, wild-eyed, then look down, mortified. We go to bed completely clothed. The mattresses sag in the middle. They're almost hammocks. All we need are trees, springtime, the cocktails, and the green olives. I don't sleep. The migraine has settled in. I sit on the edge of my bed. Something is pinching the back of my neck. I scratch and find a bedbug. I squish it with my fingers. It stinks. Will I be able to forget that odor of blood and rotten hay? My brother is awakened by the noise and bothered by the smell. I go down the hall to wash my hands. The water is just a dribble. The washbasin, broken; the cracks are filled with crud. I return to the room and sit back down on the edge of my bed. Although feeble, the light is enough for me to spot two more bedbugs on the pillow. I shake it. They fall; I squash them with my shoe. My brother joins the hunt for the smelly little bugs. For the first time all day, we laugh, even though we feel like crying over our fate — because after those wretched policemen delivered the summons to our house, my parents fell ill.

One day, just like that, men come knock at your door in

the name of the government, you don't dare verify their identity, they've come for a simple routine verification of documents. "We just have a few things to clear up with your husband," they explain; "he'll be back in an hour or two, don't worry." And then days go by and the husband does not come home. Despotism and injustice are so pervasive that everyone lives in fear. My father dreams of a system like the one in the Scandinavian countries and often talks to us about Sweden, Denmark, and democracy. He also likes America, where even if someone assassinates the presidents, revenge is not taken on the entire population. "John Kennedy died; his murderer was shot. That's all!" he said to me one day.

In the middle of the night, I begin to feel tired. My head feels hot, I'm sweating. I open the window; mosquitoes fly in by the dozens. I close it. I try to think about a lush green meadow with me sitting on a bench chatting with friends; in the distance I see a girl in a summery dress coming toward me . . . it's a dream. A fresh bedbug bite startles me. I decide to get up. I rummage through my bag and take out the cookies my mother made. I eat two of them. Crumbs fall to the floor. Ants, on the alert, come running. It's amusing to watch them. They entertain me. My brother has managed to get back to sleep; he's snoring. I whistle but that doesn't help: he changes position and keeps snoring. I study him carefully and notice the beginning of a bald spot. He's twelve years older than I am. He is a generous and cheerful man.

He got married when very young to a cousin. He finds politics interesting, but like my father, he's careful when he tackles sensitive subjects. He speaks in metaphors, mentions no names, but everything he thinks is written on his face. He is the one who explained to my parents that this summons for military duty was a punishment. My mother began to cry. "What has my son done to be punished? Why shut him up in a barracks? Why ruin his youth and destroy his health, and mine as well?" My father told her, "You know perfectly well why, he meddled in politics!" My mother, indignant: "What's this 'politics'? Is it a crime?" Before my astonished eyes, my father then launched into a lecture: "In Arabic, *politics* is *Siassa*, which comes from the verb *sassa* meaning to direct, to lead an animal, a mare or a donkey, for you must know how to guide the animal so that it gets where you want it to go. To engage in politics is to learn how to control people. Our son tried to learn this profession, he failed, is being punished for it, would have been congratulated in another country, but in ours he is permanently discouraged by being made to regret having wandered into a domain reserved for those who have the means to exercise power and who do not put up with those who contest this. There, it's quite simple. Our son made a mistake: he strayed into an area that does not belong to us."

Actually, he was trying to convince himself of what he was saying. My father abhors injustice. All his life he has denounced it, has fought against it as best he could. He knows that in this country, battling injustice can end quite badly. He'd been traumatized by the arrest and imprisonment of his nephew, who had dared to say in public that "corruption in this country begins at the top and goes all the way down to the doorman." Three days after going to see his nephew in prison, he was visited by two men who bombarded him with questions. At some point, one of them said, "You have children, boys, don't you?" My father understood instantly: he had to keep his head down. It made him sick. That evening, he had a fever and went to bed without a word. The next day, he called my older brother and me together to tell us, "Be very careful: no politics—this isn't Denmark, also a monarchy, but here it's the police who rule, so think of my health and especially of your mother's, her diabetes might get worse, so no meetings, no politics . . ."

We replied that in any case the powers-that-be could hurt us even if we avoided politics. We live in a system where everything is under control. Fear and suspicion are pre-installed. A cousin of my father's who frequented the Information Bureau warned him that I'd been seen having coffee with a leader of the student movement in Rabat. Having a coffee! A crime already noticed and archived. As for me, at the time I had absolutely no idea of the extensive security network in Morocco. I busied myself with the Ciné-Club in Tangier with a complete feeling of impunity. I saw nothing political about the club at all. The very day after we showed Sergei Eisenstein's *Battleship Potemkin*, however, I am summoned by the police. I'm fifteen years old and quaking, because it's the first time I've set foot in a police station.

The guy, maybe an officer, says to me, "Do you know this film is an incitement to rebellion?"

I'm speechless. Then I get a grip.

"But, not at all, monsieur. This film portrays a historic event that has nothing to do with our situation, it's a work of art. Eisenstein is a great cinematographer, you know."

"Don't feed me guff, I know about Eisenstein. I once wanted to work in film production—I'd even registered at the Institut des hautes études cinématographiques in Paris, but my father died in an accident, so I had to interrupt my studies, and since the police were recruiting, I signed on. Right, listen up: you're lucky I love movies. By the way, what's the next show at the Ciné-Club?"

"Ingmar Bergman's *The Virgin Spring.*"

"Very good choice. That one, at least, isn't political!"

■

By five in the morning, I'm nodding off. I no longer feel the bedbugs, mosquitoes, and so forth. The ants have disappeared. I fall asleep. No dream, no nightmare. At eight, my brother awakens me. We have to go. We eat breakfast in the café next door. Terrible coffee, but excellent mint tea, some fritters. "Careful," my brother tells me; "this cooking oil must be a year old!" It's not as noxious as the bedbugs. The fritters remind me of my childhood in the Medina, the "old city" part of Fez. Once a week, on the day we went to the hammam,[2] on our way home my father would buy us fritters for our breakfast. We'd dip them into a bowl of honey. It was unforgettably delicious. There were crumbs and dead bees in the honey pot. My brother and I would have fun cleaning out the pot, laughing and licking our fingers.

■

A beggar holds out his hand; I give him my fritters. He devours them, another beggar arrives, I give him my glass of tea; he tells me he'd prefer a cup of coffee. Bees and flies whirl around our heads. Meknès is waking up. A mint seller passes by shouting, "Good and fresh!" It's the mint of Moulay Idriss Zerhoun, the patron saint of Volubilis, near Meknès.[3] After that long and horrible night, I'm ready to brave anything.

We look for a taxi to go to El Hajeb, a half hour's drive away. People are waiting, beggars roam around, a barefoot boy picks up a cigarette stub from the ground and gets chased by a bigger boy. Some lost tourists are being pestered by a swarm of fake guides, whom a policeman chases away with reproaches: "Shame on you! You're making our country look bad!" Someone points out to him that the country's image is fairly lousy any way you look at it, from the inside or out, then runs away. "I know you!" the flic yells threateningly, "I know where you live, I'll get you — you insult the country and its king, you'll see, you'll pay dearly for that!" He begins shouting our patriotic slogan: "*Allah, Al Watan, Al Malik!*" God, the Nation, the King.

The crowd is laughing; the policeman now seems a little crestfallen.

A taxi arrives. People rush over. The flic calls for order, then tells my brother, "Get in, you're not from around here, right?"

So we're now scrunched together on the front seat. The plastic is torn, revealing foam of an indeterminate color. The driver smells of rancid butter; he's just finished breakfast. He lights a truly foul-smelling dark-leaf cigarette. Four people are in the back: an old man in a maroon djellaba, a peasant woman wrapped in a white haik,[4] her son, and a soldier on leave. The driver says, "Pay up." Everyone does. As we drive along, the discussion centers on the local soccer team. My brother, born in Fez, dares to defend his team, Le Mas. That casts a chill over the taxi. The passengers must be wondering if he might be crazy, vaunting the archenemy of the Meknès team. The driver changes the subject by discussing the price of tomatoes. That calms everyone down. The soldier tells him to pick up the pace a bit: "I'm going to get in trouble with Akka." Akka seems to be someone important. "You poor fellow!" the driver tells him. The old man sitting behind him chimes in: "Akka is very tough; he frightens everyone — even those who have never met him." The driver nods in agreement.

■

El Hajeb was originally a military base.[5] My brother looked up its history: Sultan Moulay Hassan, he tells me, had constructed a kasbah in this village to repel the rebel forces of a Berber tribe, the Beni M'tir. The army took over the base and made it into one of the main garrisons of the realm. It was a difficult period, the so-called *Siba*, which means at the same time revolt, panic, disorder, and chaos. My brother remarks to me in French: "You see how rich Arabic is! The word *Siba* leads you to so much history." The driver points out to him that he would do better to speak in Arabic. My brother excuses himself and says nothing more.

The driver drops us off a few yards from some military trucks. I think I see pity in the look he gives me. "May God protect you!" are his parting words. The soldier from the taxi begins to run; we see him salute an officer and disappear.

Before we proceed to the entrance gate, my brother hugs me and I can tell he is crying. He whispers, "My brother, I'm going to leave you in the hands of barbarians without even the right to know why or for how long these people will keep you here. Be brave and if you can, send us news. Write ordinary things, we'll read between the lines."

He suggests a few codes for me: "Everything's fine" means things are going badly; "Everything's perfectly fine" for "Everything's going really badly." "The food is as good as Mama's cooking" means things in that department aren't great either. Lastly, for trouble, I must write, "Spring has paid us a visit." I reassure him, then thank him for coming with me all the way to the camp gate.

LAST MOMENTS OF FREEDOM

Noon. A leaden sun. It's part of the drama I'm caught up in. My brother is not reassured: he looks all around and I see the sadness in his eyes. He must be remembering the people who disappear. A few months ago, for example, our neighbor stepped outside to speak with two men who had rung his doorbell; he'd gone off with them, and we haven't seen him since. His wife and children asked my father to help them compose some missing person notices they had then published in the newspapers. People are kidnapped by unknown men; the police investigate but never find them. That's how the father of my best friend joined the ranks of the disappeared. People see in this the dark hand of General Oufkir; others add, "The Palace has nothing to do with it." In reality, the king gives carte blanche to his faithful servant to bring order to the country. All those suspected of plotting or being about to plot against the king see their fate arbitrarily and definitively sealed by shadowy men, a kind of secret police who answer only to the general. They say Oufkir has the power to read the thoughts of others. He often arrests people who have done nothing. He was trained by the French during the war in Indochina. No scruples, no second thoughts, an imposing and callous manner. French experts taught him the most depraved techniques of torture. He's proud of that, it seems. The end justifies the means. Order and discipline before all else. A deeply lined face, a penetrating and inscrutable gaze, skin like the crater of an extinct volcano. They say that Mehdi Ben Barka died under torture: his heart gave out. He refused to answer the questions of flics who specialized in that kind of interrogation. Oufkir is said to have asked to be left alone with him. No words, no questions, but a couple of blows that knocked out a tooth. Mehdi was supposedly hauled up out of his chair and shaken so forcefully, in so tight a grip, that he could not breathe, lost consciousness, and his heart stopped. Oufkir then summoned his team back, the story goes, and ordered them to "get the bathtub ready." The corpse would have been dissolved in acid, leaving no trace of the leader of the Moroccan opposition. Mehdi Ben Barka's body has never been found.[1] The acid hypothesis seems quite plausible. At night, I would think about that man I'd never met; I felt somehow close to one of his children who must have been about my age, and wondered how he had experienced that tragedy, which had shaken the regime. All those who'd had a hand in the affair were liquidated. Only one escaped death, it seems. The Franco-Moroccan security forces had adopted the methods of the Mafia. At the time, even if General de Gaulle was horrified by what had happened, the police forces of both countries continued to collaborate. My father had not been surprised by that disappearance. I remember hearing him say quietly, after closing the window shutters, "The king could not bear being opposed by his former mathematics teacher; of course he made him disappear. Anyway, don't ever repeat what I just said! Not a word!"

What is sometimes exasperating is that my father dares to say things while at the same time admitting that he's afraid. My father is afraid. He isn't the only one. He passed that fear along to me, and I'm ashamed of it. His cousin, moreover, advised him to be very careful of what he says in public and told him that the police send fake customers into stores to worm information out of shopkeepers. So my father doesn't discuss any political topics with his clientele. Someone once came by collecting money: "You must contribute, for Palestine." My father replied, "What proves to me that this money really goes to the Palestinians?" The guy left without another word.

Whenever the press mentioned Mehdi Ben Barka, my father would always say the same thing: "Don't bother. We'll never learn the truth about that disappearance. Never."

               ■

Once more, my brother puts his arms around me. "May our parents' blessing protect you," he says, and holds me tight, as if we were never going to see each other again, adding, "But the most beautiful protection is that of God." With these words, he leaves me with a huge fellow, beefy, tall, with a shaved head. The man is polite with my brother, asking after him as if they knew one another, and glancing sympathetically at me he says comfortingly, "Go in peace, your little brother is in good hands." Then as soon as we're alone he hits me in the back and knocks me down. I stand up to find myself between two soldiers who pull me along and shove me into a dark round room with a small opening high in the wall. I lean against the rough wall. I look, carefully, at the ceiling and think I see iron hooks there. I'm convinced that it's where the condemned are hanged or tortured. I don't know what will be done with me. I'm hungry. They've kept my bag. It's hot, but at least I'm out of the sun. This room made of adobe is called a *tata*, a kind of temporary prison cell. The door is locked from the outside. Impossible to escape. The air is stifling; my thoughts grow darker and darker. Actually, they're not really thoughts, but a strange feeling that everything is now topsy-turvy, no longer in the right place: the living-room ceiling is studded with chairs, couches hang where the mirrors should be, night has been poured into day, and clocks have lost their hands; time has ceased to exist, kidnapped by fleeing convicts, while walls slide along on rails toward other walls stockpiled in a vast hangar where men are shrunk the way heads once were by faraway tribes, shrunk down to the size of rats, yes, human beings have become rats and find that normal. I turn in circles in this solitary confinement as if seeking a human hand, or my brother's face, as if I were trying not to turn into a rat, animals that have always so horrified me that at the movies I shut my eyes when they appear, that's how phobic I am about rats, moles, mice. I place my hands on the wall, reassure myself for a few seconds: I am not in a nightmare but imprisoned in a kind of cell where there are no rats and nothing is moving; the walls are solid and I'm solid too — well, almost — and in any case I must become strong and not let myself be overwhelmed by this situation.

Late that night, food is brought to me. I think I will remember all my life the suffocating odor of that heavy yellow sauce: camel fat. No meat; chunks of vegetables and some rock-hard bread. As if the flour has been mixed with chalk. I choose not to swallow anything. I drink water in a plastic glass. I curl up, try to sleep. I hear noise. I smell cheap cigarette smoke; later I'll learn that soldiers call the cigarettes Troupes. Strangely enough, I'm no longer worried. I await what will come next, gripping my forehead to relieve a migraine. I lean against the wall; a pebble hurts my back. I don't try to change position. This pain distracts me from the migraine. Headaches, I was born with them, that's how it is: I don't remember the first time I had one; it's an infirmity. I suffer and must get used to this affliction. At times it's a needle probing my head, at others a jackhammer digging holes.

I'm alone and no one comes to see me. Maybe they've forgotten me? My imagination has overtaken my thinking. I see myself in hopeless situations, like running in an infinite white space. The headache returns me to reality. I stand up and walk in sets of ten steps, I turn in circles, tell myself this is the beginning of madness, remember a black-and-white film called *The Hill*.[2] I see myself among those lost men, famished, thirsty, surrounded by mines, moving forward, stepping lightly, I'm afraid of blowing myself up. Hunger. I take a piece of hard bread. I dip it into the yellow sauce and swallow it, holding my nose. I select half a potato and wash it down with water. I almost choke. I cough. Late at night, a soldier opens the door, rushes at me, drags me out by the arm and off to see the colossus who'd received me earlier.

AKKA

"My name is Akka," he tells me. "Here, I'm in charge: Chief Warrant Officer Akka, don't forget that name, it has the ring of death about it. We're going to strip everything civilian from you. Take off those city clothes. All that's over. A man here's got to be a man. No fussing with hair, pomade, perfume. Get a move on. Right, *fissa!* Onna double!"

While I'm undressing, he grabs my hair. A black mop of which I'm very fond. It's the era of long hair, of rock and the Twist.

"Don't leave a single one," he tells the soldier. "He's got to learn, the punishment begins with the hair."

"Sir, yes Sir!"

The soldier is trembling. And me, I wonder if I'm going to tremble as well, or faint, laugh, or fight, yell, scream, or shut up and let myself be shorn like a lamb.

Akka leaves. I put on a maroon sweater with short sleeves and pants that are too long. I'm given sandals. They're too big. I try to walk, they flap. The soldier, shorter than I am, grabs me firmly and sits me down on a wobbly stool, saying, "We'll see later about the size of the clothes." He has stopped shaking, and I sense the feeling of superiority his power now gives him. He takes out a pair of scissors and begins cutting off my hair, which falls on my lap, on the floor. There's a lot of it. I cry silently. I look at this pile of hair and wait for what will come next. The soldier sprinkles my head with water, takes out a razor, slips in a blade and begins shaving my skull. It hurts. A drop of blood slides down my cheek. I don't say anything. The blade must have been used a few times before. He says reassuringly that I'm the tenth fellow he's shaved that evening. He takes his time, sweeping the blade back and forth, leaving the odd cut here and there. I don't move. I smell his strong odor of perspiration. I realize that for him that stink "makes a man." Everything about him reeks. When he leans toward me, his bad breath envelops me, leaves me a bit dizzy. I venture to ask him if there are showers in the camp. He replies that he prefers to go once a week to the hammam.

After half an hour, the martyrdom is over. The smell of sweat and dirty clothes is nauseating. Wish I could vomit, yet my stomach is almost empty. I don't dare run my hand over my scalp. I sit there, my head hanging. The soldier returns and tells me that I'll sleep in the tata that night while awaiting my assignment. He must be my age, a peasant who had no choice but to join the army. I ask him his name.

"Private, Platoon 3." He collects his gear, spits on the floor, and goes off.

This soldier, whom I nickname Hajjam, speaks Arabic poorly. He must be a Berber.[1] He returns, spits on the floor again, and tells me that he's lost the cigarette butt he quickly stubbed out when Akka showed up. He looks everywhere, but

finds no trace of it. I'd offer him a whole pack of American cigarettes, but I don't smoke, and anyway this isn't the moment for
cadging favors. He takes off again, cursing at city people, and
slams the door. Now what do I do with my new situation? Accept it. Difficult. At twenty, one doesn't simply accept things,
one challenges them. I think back to my first political meeting.
The year of my baccalaureate. I was discovering a world I knew
slightly through my reading and certain films, and this world was
boring, so boring. I'd felt like walking out. I didn't have that courage. The presence of my comrades weighed heavily in the bal-
ance. To be labeled a coward or a traitor . . . No, never. A fellow
named Faouzi didn't hesitate, though: he stood up and left, saying, "Good luck, this isn't for me." I should add that he was ill
and had to take medicine every four hours. He had an excuse, I
didn't. I could have announced, "I'm in love, I'm going off to my
sweetheart," and they would have just ripped me to shreds. That's
what I should have done. But my lack of courage plus my doubts
didn't help me there. Changing the world (on our minor scale)
was vital for me, I who had read Rimbaud and a few quotations
from Marx. I set aside my fears and stayed at that meeting, which
lasted hours. So many words, pretty phrases, promises, and then,
nothing. There was also a guy who'd come from Rabat who must
have been three or four years older than us. He was in charge
of setting up local headquarters in Tangier. A politician through
and through. We began the meeting with a minute of silence in
memory of Mehdi Ben Barka, who had been his friend. The man
knew how to speak, explain, convince, but when he left I was un-

able to sum up what he'd said. Short, gaunt, the kind of man who devotes his life to a cause because outside of that he'd be good for nothing. I realized that much later. *He* will not be punished. He will not be among the ninety-four men "punished by the king." He was practicing politics officially, he had the backing of a party and probably influential support as well. We, we were the cattle.

■

Akka comes by again. I see him looming, huge, like those monsters encountered in horror movies. He looks me up and down, says, "There, you're shedding your civilian status, tomorrow you'll be a soldier."

No desire to become a soldier. I say nothing. I sense that one doesn't argue with this kind of brute.

"We're going to make a man of you! No bolitics here" (he constantly massacres French), "you were doing bolitics that's why you've come, but no pro'lem, we'll fix you. Akka has more than one sleeve for his tricks . . . You unnerstan' that?"

I don't reply. I leave and look for the tata. They all look alike. Akka rejoins me and begins to chat as if we were friends. He talks about Indochina, his great exploits, the intelligence of the "Chinese"—because to him all Asians are Chinese.

"Tricky devils, they're small as rats, they run fast, you don't see them, and then they leap at you and cut your throat. I killed lots of Chinese. They were all over the place. At night when I went into my tata, I'd look under the bed 'case they were hiding there. I'm the one built these tatas here. That's what I got out of Indochina. Colonel François taught me plenty. A tremendous man. He liked killing the Chinese too. One day he was recalled, sent to Algeria to kill our brothers. Ever since then, I don't like him anymore. Me, for revenge, I helped out our Algerian brothers. All that's bolitics."

.

In the tata I sleep on the bare floor. In any case, there's no bed, but I could have spread out my clothes and slept on them. I'm so tired I fall asleep right away. I don't have a single dream.

Reveille is at six. I smell something that from afar resembles coffee. Dirty water, hot and tasteless. The bread is as hard as yesterday's. Luckily there's a portion of Laughing Cow cheese. I swallow it and lick the paper.

I feel that I have shrunk. Without my hair, I feel stunted, crushed: a bedbug, a plaything for louts. Shorn like a sheep, like someone condemned to death. I remember the story of Samson and Delilah and the power vested in the hero's hair. No more hair, no more strength. I admit this, I've become someone else and must preserve that status or else I'm screwed. What happens to me concerns a different person: I'm a straw man, a stand-in, a shadow, a phantom. I must feel nothing and above all resent nothing; I must not think but accept what happens lightly. I keep telling myself: it isn't me, it isn't me. I rub my hand over my scalp, finding scabs of crusted blood. Poor soul, they massacred him. That's enough — I'm not talking about myself anymore, the other one is here: the hand that glides over the skull is not mine and neither is the skull. I'm busy distancing myself from me, pitching and rolling heavily, drifting toward other waters, I'm no longer there, I'm acting out a farce for myself, a drama in which it's best to laugh and I run, striving to escape my skin, which hangs on . . . I'm punched in the back. It's Hajjam, telling me, "Medecal exum rat away."

MEDICAL EXAM

The doctor, a young Frenchman, is examining the latest recruits. He's in a foul mood. Irritated not with us but with his
military bosses. I strip bare; he examines me, notices a malfor-
mation of one of my testicles. He asks me questions. Sometimes
I have pain in my left ball. "You must go to the hospital," he says,
and writes down the word *epididymis*. He decides I should be released. He stamps a form and signs it: exempted. Magic word.
All recruits dream about it. In Arabic it's pronounced *xza* and it's
enough to let you know you're free.

"Go home. You're not fit for service."

Poor man! He must not know what goes on in this camp. I
don't say anything. I get dressed again. I leave smiling. I have an
official document allowing me to go back home. The business
with my testicle doesn't bother me. I don't feel a thing. Thanks to
this screwed-up ball, I'll be rescued from the camp.

On the way to the captain's office, I meet Akka. I think, He's
everywhere, he knows everything, he controls everything. I'm
afraid.

"Where're you going?"

"To see Captain Allioua."

"Why?"

"Because the doctor told me to."

"He gave you a paper?"

"Yes."

"Show me."

He takes the paper upside down, turns it right side up, and says, "Oh, you, 'xza'?"

I tell him I don't know.

"Go see the captain, he'll be happy to have a 'xza' this morning."

Captain Allioua is a man from the North, from Souk-el-Arba, I think. He's the one who says so: "We're almost neighbors, you from Tangier and me from Souk-el-Arba." He seems courteous, a fellow of good family, one can tell he's been educated, well brought up, and I wonder what he's doing in the army. He talks to me about his town and his grandmother, who is from the Fez area. I can't think why he's telling me all this. Then he comes over to me and speaks more sternly.

"Give me the doctor's paper. Ah, you're 'xza'! It's good, that is! You'll be able to go back home, you're sure lucky. 'Xza'! And yet you're rosy-cheeked, look like a stout fellow—but if you're 'xza,' then you're 'xza.' They're rare, the 'xza' guys! It makes me happy to actually see a real 'xza' because there are malingerers, little cheats who try to pass for crazy, but I'm not fooled, I send them to a madhouse, and there they really go crazy. You, you're honest. The Frenchy doctor, he did a good job. You're 'xza'! What luck! You're pleased? Tell me how it feels to be able to escape from this little hell concocted by Chief Warrant Officer Akka, the man with the shaved head . . ."

He starts laughing uproariously, which worries me.

While he's talking, he tears the medical certificate exempting me from service at the camp into little pieces.

"You see, you're not 'xza' anymore! It's magic. A minute ago you were 'xza' and now you're not, you faggot. Go on, get out of here," he says, getting ready to kick me, "and don't let me see you here again."

Back at the tata, Akka grabs me: "You're not 'xza' now! It's not good, too bad. You're in Platoon 2. You'll be back with your little friends, the Commies, traitors, fairies . . . We'll have lots of fun. Remember the Chinese? Well, to me, you lot are little Chinese minus the courage."

PUNISHED BY HIS MAJESTY

My serial number is 10 366. I remember it even today. All those whose numbers begin with the series 10 300 are men punished by the king. Which wasn't written down or proclaimed, but the punishment, the correction, the lesson, the bringing to heel, all that is in our heads. What did we do that was so serious? Organize legally; demonstrate peacefully; call for freedom and respect; be who we were, guilty only of naïveté and idealism. It seems we're not the only ones in that situation. In Egypt, Nasser sends his Marxist opponents into the desert and hands them over to psychopaths for maltreatment.

There are two sections of us, of forty-five and forty-nine members. All of us are students, except for an important official, an agronomic engineer who wound up here after refusing a posting assigned by the Palace, and a university professor suspected of being among the organizers and leaders of the demonstrations of March 23, 1965. The rest of us belong mostly to the various committees of UNEM, a student union known for its leftist orientation. As soon as I saw Akka, I realized how deep the gulf was between us. This was nothing new: faced with compassion and intelligence, power reacts with savagery, stupidity, and degradation. I call upon my literary memories; I don't know whether I'm

faithfully reciting what I've read or inventing phrases. I think of
Dostoyevsky, Chekhov, Kafka, Victor Hugo . . .

The noncoms recruited to deal with us all speak a raggedy kind
of French, unlike their charges, and they have been ordered
to set us back on the correct path, the one determined by the
regime. To this end, the security unit of the Ministry of National
Defense has drawn up a program of abuse and humiliation. To
them, we're tough nuts. Akka and his acolytes are here to crack
us. And the dull blade that shaves our skulls is a first taste of what
His Majesty's soldiers have in store for us.

Scenes from the films of Charlie Chaplin stream through
my mind. Why is good ol' Charlie visiting me in this hole full of
dreadful soldiers? I'm laughing inside, pleased to be haunted by
the little fellow who manages to make fun of the bullies torment-
ing him. This genius has avenged millions of persecuted people
in this world. There you have it: that was his mission, his inten-
tion. Thank you Charlie.

HEAVY STONES OUT IN THE SUN

Camp Commandant Ababou, whom we have not yet seen, has decided to build, three miles to the north of the camp, a wall five hundred fifty yards long and about five yards high. A wall no one needs. An absolutely useless wall, absurd out in the fields, a wall to justify the lugging of big stones by men being punished. Why not be useful and build houses for the peasants whose homes collapse every winter after the rain? Why not truly help people who need assistance, relief?

Why indeed. I stop *thinking*. We're in the territory of the absurd: nothing to say, nothing to propose. Ababou must be proud of his lucky find, a wall for nothing, that's all it is: a wall built up, then torn down. A gratuitous exercise in mistreatment.

A truck delivers piles of dressed stones brought from somewhere outside the camp. We're given pieces of cloth, about a yard square; we put the stones on them, make a loose knot with the four corners of the material, and carry on our backs a load of up to sixty-five pounds. The trek is usually made just when the sun is at its hottest. Anyone who falls gets hit with a baton, followed by a few kicks. We have to work fast. They make us hurry along. No water to drink. No stopping. The three miles must be covered within the hour, "on the dub."

The sergeants in our escort snipe at us: "It's your fault that we're getting punished too!" We arrive, we unload. My back hurts; I stretch a little to ease the pain. A sergeant sees me, rushes over and whacks the back of my neck with his baton. I almost collapse for good. He insults me, then spits in the dirt. Silence in the ranks. The guards notice even where we look. Shirts stick to skin. Someone begs for a little water. No water! No question of going back with empty cloths, unburdened: wood and sand must be carried back. We take up new loads and head for the camp. We deliver them—and get new stones to carry off. We're allowed a small ration of water.

After one week, the wall is built, then immediately torn down. We must take the stones back to camp; trucks are waiting to return them to where they were originally piled. Once more we run, we load up and set out again, still bearing stones on our backs.

This goes on for about two weeks. Only at the end does Commandant Ababou address us all as follows:

"*Balkoum!* Attention! You're here to learn to love and respect your country. You're here to deserve life under this magnificent flag. You're here to learn and to forget. To learn to obey, serve, learn discipline, respect honor. To forget rabble-rousing, pernicious ideas, cowardice, and idleness. Arriving here, you were weaklings; leaving—if you ever do one day—you will be men, real ones, not those overgrown spoiled children raised on yogurt and imported powdered milk. Here you do not exist, you are a serial number. I have complete rights over you, and you have none. That's how it is, and anyone who doesn't like it can just step forward. I'm called Commandant Ababou. I am in charge of this camp. Everything goes through me. Chief Warrant Officer Akka here present is my second-in-command. He is me when I am not here. I do not advise you to annoy him, still less to disobey him. He knows only force, blows, barbarity that would reduce anyone at all to the level of an animal. Understood? Dismissed!"

Just before he shouts "dismissed," an unfortunate soul steps forward. The commandant beats him bloody with his baton, kicks him until he collapses, and tears into him, insulting his mother, father, and all his ancestors. The sweating commandant froths at the mouth, yelling, lost in his frenzy. Akka intervenes, managing to put an end to the suffering of the hapless fool who dared step forward in protest.

Ababou is of medium height, rather burly, a hard case with sharp, shining eyes, a firm step and unhesitating manner. He walks off as if nothing has happened. Two soldiers take the other man off to the infirmary. A couple of broken ribs and a tooth knocked out. We are frightened but not surprised. No comment necessary. Anyway, we're probably watched, overheard, and would be denounced at the slightest thought of protest. Ababou reads our minds.

We have understood the lesson. We are there to obey and be quiet, to keep our heads down and stand at attention at the snap of an order.

I look around me. We are all dismayed and paralyzed with fear. This is a feeling radically unlike any other we have known.

Here: violence, blows, blood, and perhaps death. We are surrounded by hatred and inhumanity. These soldiers must have been chosen with care; perhaps they went looking for recruits in psychiatric hospitals. How could our army be a machine to punish and brutalize? Yet Akka and his acolytes are proud of their role. I feel fear in my belly, and it will be there for a good long time. At twenty, no one wants to set his life on fire and provoke a madman capable of massacring us all. In this camp we are isolated from the world. No way to call for help, no one will hear us, nobody will come save us. Isolated camp, territory off-limits. Many families were told that we are performing our military service. But no one is fooled. Before our arrest, there was no such obligation. They invented it to disguise their attempt to reform young people a touch too lively for their taste who dared protest against unfair and immoral decisions from the National Ministry of Education. It's the first time the regime has felt challenged. The monarchy isn't used to that. We are here to set an example.

∎

The rotten grub they feed us makes me sick. So I avoid eating. Nevertheless, since yesterday I've had painful diarrhea. The most disgusting place in the camp is the toilets, the Turkish kind. A hole. Now and then a rat pops out, terrified. I scream. I hold out as long as I can to avoid that horrible latrine.

Some heed nature's call out in nature. If caught, however, they risk going to prison. We hear that the officers' mess hall has clean toilets. It's forbidden territory, surrounded by the aromas of good cooking, but we haven't the right even to pause there, still less go inside. A fellow prisoner rubs his index finger against his thumb to suggest a bribe: if we give baksheesh to the soldier at the entrance during off-hours, he'll let us shit decently, if we can hang on until the guard whistles an all-clear. We're all ready to pay to shit in peace!

Corruption reigns everywhere, including in this wretched camp. But one must be incredibly careful.

There's one fellow among us with very white skin and almost no beard. He is occasionally summoned by one of the officers, then returns an hour or two later. What does he do when he's absent for so long? Is he a spy for the officer? He refuses to answer our questions, so we decide to give him the silent treatment. One day, we suddenly understand: he gets fucked by the lieutenant. When one of us mentions it to him he starts crying like a child caught misbehaving. He cries so much that we leave him in peace. Someone even remarks, "He might be useful to us." We're still mistrustful of him, but openly sympathetic. It's nobody's fault if he likes to sleep with the lieutenant. That's his business. As long as he doesn't become a snitch.

MANEUVERS IN THE RAIN

Sembly at four o'clock. *Rivail* awakens us at three. *Paktage pri* means backpack ready, *sakado compli*—full kit—at three-thirty. Always the same orders, shouted by an illiterate corporal sent here to humiliate students, intellectuals. Today it's Hajjam, the one who shaved my scalp when I arrived. Having a head like a cue ball is part of the program. As is addressing us in ridiculous and sloppy French.

Our barracks of a hundred "soldiers" is commanded by each of us in turn. Abdenebi, a thin and intelligent fellow, takes over. He's doubtless a militant, a Communist. In any case he takes his role quite seriously, clearly displaying the discipline acquired in a Party cell. Nothing wishy-washy. He has put on a military uniform and behaves exactly like the soldiers whose mission is to make us eat dirt. He warns us, "Lights out at twenty-one hours. I want everyone standing at the foot of his bed at three. As for the rest, Corporal Hmidouch has already informed you just now." This guy knows the name of the noncommissioned officer I call Hajjam! I wonder about his surprising ability to take on the persona of a leader. Maybe Abdenebi is the kind of person who likes to give orders, to command, lead, be obeyed, brook no dissent . . .

I don't see myself leading this troop. I'm allergic to being in charge. What pleasure is there in giving orders and seeing oneself obeyed? That doesn't interest me, and at the same time I detest being ordered around. I've always loved not only freedom, but fantasy and caprice, whereas order scares me. Disorder as well. I need to feel free enough to dream, imagine, dance around in my head, break ranks, shun all labels, be unpredictable, elusive. Rimbaud's poetry opened my mind and gave me the courage to dream, but I've no talent for playing a soldier or an officer giving orders.

■

Short night. Uneasy night. Sleepless, dreamless night. I breathe slowly to relax. I imagine huge butterflies crossing a wheat field. I see a mermaid gliding delicately across the surface of the sea, a sea so calm, so blue, so beautiful. I see myself in summertime beneath an olive tree, composing poems. I reach out to touch the grass. I look up at the sky, and stars streak swiftly away. I summon the image of my fiancée and I caress her. I feel nothing. My libido is at dead zero. Then the smell of the sleepers around me brings me back to reality. Designed for about forty beds, the barracks contains well over twice that number. All these men in such a small space foul the air with thick odors. People do seem to get used to anything, so I have to put up with the suffocating stench of sweat. There's no point in complaining, anyway: this isn't a hotel or a cemetery, it's a boot camp where we are to endure both physical and psychological punishment. And because we are spoiled children, we must be ruthlessly disciplined.

Even though I and many of my comrades come from poor backgrounds, the soldiers glare at us with hatred, jealous of the simple fact that we have had some higher education.

■

Where are they taking us? Why all these preparations? We have no right to ask questions. It's forbidden to make inquiries, forbidden to speak up — this isn't a camp meeting. Gathering together is forbidden. No right to form little groups. Forbidden to sigh, to make a remark, forbidden to look annoyed, forbidden to burst out laughing. They think we're making fun of them. Our demeanor must be neutral, an attitude of submission. No discussion. Abdenebi is on the other side: he walks and talks like the career soldiers, he's acquiring a taste for this role, reviewing our ranks with an air of contempt like a real captain; he's playing, it amuses him, he is happy. He still thinks he can profit from the situation. Later I'll learn that this young man will join the army and die in the Sahara in an attack by mercenaries fighting for Algeria.

■

I ask my parents silently for their blessing, I pray to God and his Prophet, I pray to the heavens and the stars, I pray to the forests and the sea, to flowerbeds and kitchen gardens, and I count the minutes. I look neither to the right nor to the left. I am what Akka wishes me to be: a submissive soldier on the way to becoming a man! I was unaware that our parents had turned us into half-men. Akka is there to finish the job. We ought to thank him, perhaps kiss his hand, raise a statue to him in the center of the camp, but the commandant would not approve. I imagine Akka as a granite statue, set upside down on the ground, feet pointing toward the sky. I imagine his boss Ababou ordering that the sculptor be arrested and the artwork shattered into a thousand pieces. Here, we don't joke around. Here, we don't create. We don't invent. All imagination is forbidden. Here, we obey, that's it, that's all.

•

Four in the morning. We're ready. It's raining buckets. Both platoons are lined up, MAS-36 rifles at parade rest, knapsacks on our backs, weighing about twenty-five pounds. Stale bread is distributed, to be eaten on the spot with some cheese. "Chicafé," made from coffee beans and chickpea flour, is served in metal cups. Revolting. I won't risk a tongue-lashing and blows from the corporal just because the coffee is undrinkable. I drink it anyway and say nothing. My face a blank. Not even a tiny twitch. I dip the bread in the blackish liquid and swallow. A lieutenant arrives and inspects us. We remove our helmets and he runs a baton over our scalps to make sure they've been properly shaved. If they haven't, he strikes the soldier's head sharply and demands his serial number for punishment, adding, "No one puts anything over on Lieutenant Marzouk!" And I wonder, Whatever would I want to try? Fooling him? Treating him like an idiot? I would never dream of playing around with men like this, who are so insecure about their virility. Okay, you're the biggest, the best, the one with real balls. And so? So what!

We're lined up neatly under the pounding rain. Wet through. We are completely soaked. The water is running down right between shirt and skin. It's cold. We mustn't show that we're miserable, mustn't shiver, feel faint. No, we stand in the rain and we do not flinch. Now that is a soldier in the process of hominization. We are not pushovers, milksops, coddled brats, gobblers of "gazelle horn" pastries, flabby bodies wrapped in fat and smothered with affection; we are no longer fakes, see-through men.

Our humanity is rudely tested. I keep mine at the bottom of my soul. I promise myself not to give in, to resist this savagery imposed as a virtue. I think, This is ridiculous, it's all rubbish, like a really bad movie. My ideas are growing confused. A sign of deep fatigue.

I think again about our humanity. The day before, I'd spent some time reading the scribblings on the latrine walls. These soldiers suffer in silence. I noticed a few expressions more interesting than those about "the biggest dick in El Hajeb": "this isn't a life"; "I dream about living"; "I'm cutting off a finger to get out of here"; "may God curse the army"; "Akka is Satan"; "Akka fucks the commandant"; "no future"; "hell is here"; "to die . . ."; "jump on a bomb"; "long live liberty"; "better to croak than give up your ass"; "strawberries and sugar"; "fuck it!"; "God is great"; "God has forgotten us"; "Ababou is a shrimp" . . .

■

Another lieutenant shows up. "Balkoum!" He explains to us that we'll be participating in some maneuvers. Our side is the green group. We have to beat the red group. The fight will be tough. "Get ready for some real battles. This time there are no blanks, there were none in the armory, so watch out! This isn't a game. This is serious. This is how you become a man." They certainly know a whole lot about what is and isn't a man.

Before leaving, he adds these last chilling remarks: "The law permits a fatality rate of 2 percent. In your case, it can rise to 5 percent. You've been warned. Repeat the Shahada: 'There is no God . . . but God . . . and Muhammad is his Prophet.'" We repeat this profession of faith that all Muslims must make at the approach of death. This dramatic scene has been well crafted. The possibility of death at the end of this long day has us all petrified.

Silence in the ranks. I'm scared. The rain keeps falling harder. Every stitch of me is wet. I feel the water run down my back, over my buttocks, come back out over my feet. I'm quaking. To die in the rain for nothing. Wanting a warm drink, even hot water, that would do it.

At five o'clock we set out. The sky is black, the rain our constant companion. We walk for two hours. We're far from the camp. We reach the mountains. They tell us that the enemy is on the other side and can attack at a moment's notice. Our lieutenant decides that we will attack first. He sets an example, throwing a grenade that explodes. Shots ring out. It's war. I'm more and more certain that these maneuvers are a trap so that the army can get rid of us. We look at one another; some comrades agree with me, while others—the "political" prisoners—assure us that they'd never be able to get away with that. No time to think, speak, we have to run and hide, to shoot in any direction whatever. It's still raining. I think of a song by that master chansonnier Jacques Brel in which he talks about death in the winter. Dying, for whom, for what? That thought puts me in a frenzy: I set off running at top speed, I fall and get up, keep running, and stash myself behind a tree. A pal joins me. He says it's a game, that the bullets are blanks. I'm not sure. Why warn us about the possibility of 5 percent of us dying? They've got the law on their side. Our families know nothing of what we're going through; they think we're doing the usual military service of civilized countries. They have no idea of the masquerade the king's army has found to eliminate us. A few more shots are fired. Our other companions join us. We're told someone has been wounded. I look at my friend: "A real bullet, pal!"

At that point, we decide that we won't let ourselves get picked off like sitting ducks. Toward ten o'clock, fifteen minutes' rest. They give us coffee and bread. The lieutenant tells us that the other side has a few wounded and perhaps one dead. He's using a walkie-talkie. Speaking in code. The rain has stopped. We're floundering in mud. The backpack is even heavier from the rain.

Fear has become a strange courage. As I walk I compose a poem in my head. I promise myself to write it down if I survive. I don't know why, but in those terrible moments I think of the girl I love and who left me. I forgive her and would like to see her one last time. To hold her, feel her close, bury my face in her lovely long hair, breathe in her perfume, kiss the eyes she would close when she gave herself, and above all, I would say nothing: no words, no reproaches. I'd like to lay her down on the grass and cover her body with kisses, knowing that it would be the last time we'd see each other. The idea haunts me. A last rendezvous, a last kiss, one last time, the way the condemned man awaits the sunrise to advance blindfolded to his fate. I feel tears welling up, but I hold them back. Who hasn't dreamed one day of experiencing a last embrace, the final sentence in a love story that is banal — and yet so moving?

I decide to be content with memories, to spread them out before me and contemplate them sadly. Disturbing images invade my little scenario. It's her, always her, in the arms of another, laughing gaily, running along the empty beach of Tangiers, letting down her hair before falling onto the sand, waiting for her lover to come take her. I drive all that out of my head and turn toward a different horizon.

My head is full of things from books and movies, filling me with energy and the desire not to get myself killed. I'm wiped out. All strength gone. I collapse. I'm lugged away and left sitting against a tree. A sergeant shows up, calls me a wimp; I don't reply. Another sergeant gives me an orange tablet to chew, it must be vitamin C. I get up and follow the others.

Noon, lunch break. Sardines in oil, Laughing Cow, and a tablet of bitter chocolate. I check the expiration date on the sardine tin: well past, of course. I have the feeling I'm in for a stomachache. "Given how long we've been eating food too rotten even for pigs," my neighbor tells me, "we've got to be immune." He belches and polishes off my sardines. Then there's a great disturbance; something serious seems to have happened. Maybe some soldiers really have been killed. A doctor's jeep—we can tell from his red beret—flashes by. Real bullets. Real death.

■

The maneuvers end at around four. Cease firing! Back to camp! But in what condition?

Wiped out. Soaked to the bone, starving, brutalized, pushed to our last limits of resistance. We have no other clothes to change into. We strip and hang our fatigues to dry in the barracks. Everyone's shaken, apprehensive. At rock bottom. Abdenebi calls the roll. Two soldiers are missing. He starts over. Full assembly. One of the two men was in the latrines, he arrives clutching his belly. Abdenebi lashes into him viciously, then goes to inform the lieutenant, who reports to Chief Warrant Officer Akka, who murmurs into the ear of Commandant Ababou. A man is missing. I don't know who it is. Perhaps he took advantage of the mayhem during the battle to run away.

■

That evening, full camp assembly, the punished men and the others, the volunteers and professional soldiers. As in a performance, all is organized by a masterly hand. Silence in the ranks. The sky is black. The trees utterly still. The surrounding mountains are asleep. Commandant Ababou arrives, followed by his lieutenants. Akka steps off to one side to observe the scene. A leaden silence. A menacing darkness. The air is immobilized. Nothing moves. Suddenly a crow flies over the courtyard.

Attention! A speech from on high:

"The maneuvers were a success. Only five wounded and three dead. But there are no wounded" (he hammers out these words), "there are no dead. No one died, you hear me, no one died today. Dismissed! A hot dinner will be served to you."

■

We never learned who those wounded and dead men were. As for the fellow hurt in our group, he disappeared. Word was that he was moved to the Mohammed V military hospital in Rabat.

From that day forward, I understand who Commandant Ababou really is and what he's willing to do. Impulsive, bad-tempered, determined, heartless. A callous and cold-blooded soldier who aspires to become a legend.

He is a time bomb.

■

I ask my brother at home to send me a paperback book, the biggest one possible. Three months later, I receive a doorstop nine hundred pages long. I go off somewhere to open it by myself: *Ulysses,* by James Joyce. My brother has added a note saying,

"There's nothing bigger. You've got at least a month's worth of reading!" It must be a novel about travel. I read the jacket copy: the story takes place during one day in Dublin, June 16, 1904. Leopold Bloom and Dedalus walk around the city . . . I wonder what it has to do with the *Odyssey*. That very evening I plunge into the doorstop. I feel lost, yet happy to have a friend, a new companion. I don't understand where the novel is going, I read it slowly, as if it had been written for lovers of literature deprived of their liberty. When I think back about this book now, I remember the emotions of stolen moments, of secret reading, and the joy, the pleasure I felt. I didn't really care about understanding what I was reading: I was reading to read. I adored devouring those pages, so well written, in those surroundings utterly devoid of any trace of culture and intelligence.

MOHAMMED V HOSPITAL

Rumors are going around. Ababou is in hot water. Akka as well. The mistreatment has gone too far. It seems that General Driss Ben Omar is not happy. And that there were more than three dead. Our food has been slightly improved. No more rotten meat in camel fat. We even had some chicken for the first time. It smelled a bit but was edible. Someone in the mess hall told us he'd never seen that before: "The army buys products no longer fit for consumption—I even think they get them free, and the proof they're dangerous is that we get batches of drugs to add to the cooking pots." With our grub money the commandant must be buying cases of wine, fine imported foods, crates of fresh fruits and vegetables. Then he calls in some *Chikhates* and throws parties on the backs of the punished men.[1]

We know that our health is of little importance. We are here to follow orders and to regret what we did in civilian life. But what did we do wrong? Protest, oppose, demonstrate? We didn't break shop windows, didn't loot or steal, we simply cried out against inequality, injustice, repression. As my father says, "We're not in Denmark." No, we're in a beautiful country monopolized by a king and his henchmen. They are many and varied, these people who serve the monarchy by groveling on their bellies, forsaking all dignity, and they want all our people to grovel with them, like a doormat or at best a rug on which the monarch wipes his feet.

"I was twenty. I won't let anyone say that it's the best time of one's life." Like a neon sign flashing on and off, the opening of Paul Nizan's *Aden Arabie* keeps running through my thoughts.[2]

Yes, I'm twenty and I don't know if I'll ever get out of this hell. I say that over and over, I think of my parents who have had no news of me, I think of the woman I love who must now be with someone else. And yet our meeting was a *coup de foudre*, a marvel, a passion. We were about the same age; she was just six months younger. We loved each other in frustration, for we had to be careful. People talk, and gossip maliciously.

One day while we were kissing under a tree in a field outside the city, some kids began throwing stones and insulting us. I protected her as we fled. A week before my arrest, her father came to see mine, and my father often told me what he said: "Your son is seeing my daughter. It's one thing or the other: either this is serious and we draw up the contract, or it's a passing fancy and tell your son not to come near my daughter again." Her father was tall, rather imposing, and exceedingly solemn. I convinced my parents to offer the marriage proposal. Papers were signed. We were officially engaged. For the first time we strolled in the city holding hands, and we had orange juice on the terrace of the Café Pino. A strange absence . . . An odd thought: I miss her, yet she doesn't belong to me.

■

We must surely be thought of as dead or disappeared. If things keep on like this, I've planned to die. It's the first time suicide has crossed my mind. I remember the words of Christian Pacoud, a poet who said he lived "with death slung across my chest." An idea to keep from going around in circles: consider the right to kill oneself before humiliation becomes unbearable. I know that Islam forbids taking one's own life. All religions condemn suicide. An act of defiance against the Creator. A challenge to God. My religious fervor is quite faint. No one here talks about Islam. There is no mosque in the camp. Of course: we're considered miscreants. We're not good citizens: daring to protest is like daring to be an atheist or agnostic.

On the way to training exercises one day, I saw a soldier meant to die, buried in the sand up to his neck, facing the sun. The sight terrified and revolted me. What had this wretch done to deserve that agony? He disobeyed Akka, that's all we knew.

The heat is horrid. I'm dizzy. I stumble and get up again. Tell myself I have to carry on. That unfortunate soldier hadn't the strength left even to cry.

■

I fall ill. High fever. Shivering. At the infirmary, they give me some pills. A friend from Tangiers is in desperate shape. He's been taken to Rabat. My fever passes but leaves me with diarrhea. No appetite. I eat only bread dunked in the awful coffee. I have acquired the bad habit of eating really fast. Gulping rather than eating. I have myself put on the sick list a few days in a row to avoid work. After the fatigue duty with the stones, they came up with a painting assignment: whitewashing all the tatas. I feel weaker and weaker. With vertigo. I have trouble staying on my feet for long. I figure I'll die without ever seeing my parents and brothers again, without speaking to my fiancée, without glimpsing the sea. I'll die on a bed of stones . . . It's because I'm sick that I'm dwelling on my fiancée and her betrayal. At twenty, one doesn't count on eternal love. She was too pretty, too lively, a little too flighty to wait patiently. It's through absence that one discovers the intensity of love or its ravages. But I mustn't let myself sink into melancholy and despair.

My pal from Tangiers comes back, restored to health. He tells me that the hospital in Rabat is a comfy refuge. I get thinner. With intermittent fevers. I consult a doctor and end up with the French one I first saw, who doesn't recognize me. I remind him of my visit, the business with the left testicle. Then he remembers. I tell him about the ill treatment and abuse that victimize us. He lowers his voice: "I know." I ask if he can send me to the Mohammed V hospital. He makes a phone call, then writes me a prescription and a letter. "Tomorrow, in theory, you're leaving." I can remember his face but not his name anymore.

I travel from El Hajeb to Rabat in a military truck delivering some kind of merchandise. I don't ask any questions. The driver smokes nonstop. When he isn't smoking, he's chatting in Berber with a friend. Me, I'm sitting on a crate having trouble staying upright. I can see the landscape through a hole in the canvas top. Cows and sheep are in the fields; I envy them. They're free. My stomach hurts. I vomit all over the merchandise. The driver's pal curses me. I say nothing.

Once at the hospital, the driver and his pal leave me in the truck, telling me not to move. An hour later they return with an orderly who signs some papers. I get out and into the hands of that man in white, who offers me coffee and some bread dipped in olive oil.

"Did you go on the recent maneuvers?" he asks me.

"Yes."

"You're lucky, you didn't die!"

No, I didn't die, and it was indeed a question of luck, a stroke of good fortune. I feel free even though I know I have no right to. In front of a desk, I see a woman in white talking on the phone and laughing. I wish I could call my mother, just hear the sound of her voice, reassure her, tell her everything's fine . . . The orderly understands what I want.

"Mustn't dream of that, my friend, you're not allowed to use the telephone, and neither am I, actually."

Ever since that day, I've had great respect for that apparatus: I researched the man who invented it and I dream of writing his story. The inventor of the telephone was an Italian named Antonio Meucci, not Alexander Graham Bell, as we are taught. What does it matter, it wasn't an Arab! I remember my mother calling that thing set up close to her bed "the little black slave."

"I adore its music," she used to tell me, "even if this tiny trickster doesn't always bring good news."

■

I'm reborn. I come back to life. Arriving in this military hospital looking out on the Atlantic Ocean is a liberation. My pain is gone. Even my migraine has given up. I'm an interesting case. This business with the testicle intrigues a doctor, who examines me, palpates my balls, asks me if I was ever violently kicked in the scrotum. I say yes. I don't exactly remember. He keeps me under observation. I have X-rays, lab tests, they treat my ear infections, they hover over me: I've become a research project. I spend two weeks being spoiled and ask for paper and a pencil. I write my first compositions on the hospital's prescription forms. There are six of us in the room. My neighbor to the left is dying. He's so pale, so weak. I notice tufts of his gray hair on the pillow. He sleeps with his mouth open. Now and then, a moan. An orderly arrives and looks around at us: "He won't last long; let me know when his soul comes out." The expression surprises me. I begin to watch him and keep my eyes open to catch the soul coming out. I stare fixedly at him. Nothing comes out. I get tired and close my eyes. Suddenly, I hear a cry, swiftly stifled. That's it: the soul came out but I missed it.

At the end of these two weeks a sergeant comes to get me. We travel in a jeep. Once out of Rabat, he begins to ask me questions. I figure I've got one of those soldiers from Military Intelligence. Perhaps. He wants to know everything: the reasons for the punishment, what I think of the army, if I would be interested in enlisting the way he did, was I going to get married, what weapon I prefer, do I like ironing gray shirts, what was the illness that landed me in the hospital, do I have a passport, what countries would I like to visit . . .

I reply with indifference. I don't feel like talking with him. At the end, he says, "Ah, you're suspicious of me, you think I'm a secret agent who's pumping you for information? In our department, when we want something, we don't beat about the bush: wire up the balls, and everyone talks."

"I know."

"What do you mean, you know?"

"Some friends were tortured by the police in Casa."

"Why?"

"They never had the slightest idea; the torture was applied randomly and the flics love to let you know that."

"You're involved in politics?"

"No."

"Then why does your serial number begin with 10 300? That's a code for us. We hate politicals and professors."

We stop on arrival at Meknès, and the sergeant suggests having a beer. I tell him I don't drink. He gives me to understand that I'm supposed to buy him one and while I'm at it a pack of American cigarettes as well. I spend the little bit of money I have with me. I order a lemonade and we get back on the road. He tells me something I'd already suspected.

"You know, so that you all don't get hard-ons anymore,

they put something in the coffee, I think it's called brou, bro—
anyway, it's something like that . . ."

"Bromide?"

"Yes, that's it, it prevents fucking. But Lieutenant Zéroual,
he takes advantage to screw the youngsters, the ones who've just
joined the army. He's a really strong guy, you'd best not answer
him when he says anything. Keep this between us, don't start
people thinking there's army guys sharing their butts. Here we
look down on 'bottoms' . . ."

With or without bromide, my libido is nowhere. Nothing.
Not the slightest twinge. Everything here is anti-erotic unless
you're inclined to boys, like Lieutenant Zéroual, who's probably not the only one in the camp humping the new recruits, but
that's hush-hush. In the barracks, there's a big dope who looks
like a Volkswagen Beetle (an astonishing resemblance, you see
him immediately as that low-slung car with the flattened nose),
and we know he masturbates noisily but has trouble coming. He
gets pissed off and, as if he were alone in a bathroom, starts rag-
ing at the army, accusing it of castrating him.

When I think of my ex-fiancée, when I envision myself
caressing her breasts, thighs, kissing her, it no longer has any
effect. I can't get it up. I don't even feel like masturbating. We
never talk about this among ourselves.

The sergeant enjoys the blond tobacco cigarettes, exclaim-
ing with every puff what a pleasure they are. The smoke gives me
a headache. When we arrive in camp, I see Akka, his baton under

his arm, waiting in front of the gate. While I am getting out of the jeep, he runs the tip of the baton over my scalp and says:

"Going to have to shave all that hair. And right away, too. Then you come see me, on the dub."

I ask a neighbor to help me shave. The showers are closed at night. I wash up as best I can. I go see Chief Warrant Officer Akka.

"Tell me, what's your illness?"

"I've got a malformed testicle."

"Because a ball's fucked up, you take off for a vacation in Rabat!"

He shouts, stands up then sits down, rages, and perspires.

"Right, if I told you to come see me, it's because the commandant would like to ask you some questions. You're a philosophy student, right? Oh, I bet that's hard, that is! I don't know what's got into the commandant, but I'm supposed to bring him any of you punished guys who've had some education. You're lucky, I don't know why, but he must like you, otherwise I'd have made you pay for that two-week vacation 'cause here we don't like shirkers—you know, cheaters . . ."

When I get back to the barracks, everyone wants to hear about Rabat—if the nurses are pretty, if the food is high quality . . . One fellow we'd nicknamed the Weasel because of his long slouchy physique asks me how much to pay the doc to get sent to the hospital. "Nothing," I tell him. "You just have to be actually sick. The doctor does his job, he's a French guy doing his alternative military service here, and in theory he's not aware of our status or the treatment targeting us, and in any case you mustn't talk to him about it, he's in a tough spot, he's still an outsider . . ."

A few days after my return, we're awakened by unusual noises. It's a wedding, or something like that. Maybe Commandant Ababou is celebrating his promotion. We don't know a thing, but he's rumored to now be a lieutenant colonel. That calls for a party. Which would explain the Berber music for the Chikhate dancers, and even off in our barracks the noise reaches us so clearly that we can't fall back asleep. We also hear laughter, shouting, and ululations. Someone says, "The commandant is celebrating his thirty-third birthday." And it must be a party with plenty to drink. Toward the end of the day, black limousines were seen delivering well-dressed men, but no one saw the Chikhates arrive. Akka must have brought them in through a hidden door. The aroma of the *méchoui* mutton floats in the air.[3] Ababou and his friends, all superior officers, are having a great time and don't even know that not too far away ninety-four young students are starving and mired in depression. The next day, crates of empty whiskey bottles are piled at the camp gate. Perhaps they put them there to taunt us.

AN EVENING CHEZ ABABOU

One evening after dinner, I'm summoned with two other companions by Commandant Ababou. He lives in a pleasant house with a garden that has a couple of trees. We enter; one of the soldiers on guard duty installs us in the living room on some fake leather sofas and brings us tea. I have never tasted such sweet, strong, delicious mint tea. Everything takes on unfamiliar dimensions. The sofa seems so soft to me, so comfortable, that my skin feels flattered. We look at one another without a word. On the wall: a portrait of Hassan II as the leader of the Royal Armed Forces, next to a black-and-white photograph of Mohammed V.[1]

Ababou arrives. We stand up, at attention. He gestures for us to sit down, removes his gloves, places a dossier on the table, gets comfortable, and starts right in:

"Which of you can tell me something about Lenin?"

We're scared stiff. Talking about Lenin in the house of our tormentor, the one who abuses and humiliates us. A trap? A provocation?

It's so bizarre to go from our barracks, truly a stable for animals, to a comfortable house in order to talk about Lenin! I turn toward Abbas, the militant Communist.

Abbas, a disciplined man, begins to situate the life and actions of Lenin within the context of the Russian Revolution, and talks about Karl Marx, mentioning his German background. He evokes the class struggle, the end of man's exploitation of man, etc.

Ababou listens attentively, then interrupts:

"What does he say about religion?"

"It's Marx who says it's 'the opium of the people.'"

"He could have thrown in soccer, too!" exclaims Ababou, laughing.

Then he asks me a question that sounds like an indictment.

"You, you led a student movement, you organized strikes at the university, and you pushed kids to demonstrate, didn't you? Don't interrupt me when I'm talking. So, you're an agitator, you're familiar with civilian guerrilla tactics, you know what the Vietnamese did, what the Cubans did . . ."

I remain silent.

"Are you going to answer?" he yells.

Startled, I stammer some meaningless words, then pull myself together and decide to take him seriously. I think, Too bad, here goes.

"Yes, commandant: the minister of national education, Youssef Belabbès, issued an administrative memorandum that prevented students more than seventeen years old from advancing to the second level in our lycées, thus shunting them into vocational training. The demonstrations against this memorandum were quite peaceful in the beginning, even though strikers and workers from the Moroccan Workers' Union had joined the students. The repression, on the other hand, was very violent. There were at least fifty dead and three hundred wounded. But if the police had not fired on the crowd, I don't think we would have had the riots that followed."

My two companions look at me as if in encouragement; as for Ababou, he rises, paces back and forth, downs a glass of tea in one go, and returns to me.

"So, you're a revolutionary?"

"No, commandant, I am a poet, a dreamer. On the day of the demonstration I felt sad because I'd had an argument with my fiancée . . . so I melted into the crowd—and got beaten."

"You cried because a girl was angry at you?"

"No, commandant, I did not cry, but I was sad. That's normal, she was my first love . . ."

"What sort of a story is that? A man, a real one, never falls in love, or else he's done for . . . You think General de Gaulle was in love?"

"Yes, commandant: in love with France!"

He laughs, then asks the two others a few general questions. As we're leaving, he tells us that we'll be going to a different camp. Without revealing our destination, he simply says that it will be more comfortable than this one.

A few days later we are visited by General Driss Ben Omar, who beat back the Algerians in October 1963 in what has been called the Sand War: Algeria did not want to give Morocco back the mining city of Tindouf, annexed by France in 1934, because iron mines had been discovered there, and there were some additional problems regarding border disputes. On the day of the visit we're served a decent dinner; each of us even received an apple instead of a Laughing Cow.

This visit worries us all. Is war perhaps imminent with our Algerian neighbor? Why did the general talk about frontiers, the territorial integrity of the nation, the sacrifices we'll have to accept to defend the country?

Rumors of mobilization on the eastern borders circulate through the camp. It occurs to me that this would be the best way to get rid of hotheads and eggheads. There were ninety-four of us punished, minus the one who vanished. If they send us to the front line to fight the Algerians, we'll surely be killed right away. Good riddance! This must be another idea of that pervert Oufkir, who fired on the students in Rabat and Casablanca. The one who had us arrested and delivered into the hands of an Akka.

THE CONVOY

Early in the morning of January 1, 1967, some months after my arrival, I hear the rumble of truck engines. The noise is intense. I'm sure they're coming to get us. We'll be changing camps, we'll be lined up along the frontier with Algeria. I'm petrified, stomach aching, impossible to concentrate. I harbor no hatred for the Algerian people, I don't see why I would attack them. If I disobey I'll be shot. You can't be a conscientious objector here; here, you obey or you die. Case in point: the soldier punished this summer, buried out in the sun, died insane.

Perhaps war will be declared in the coming hours. We are not allowed radios or newspapers. When one of us is occasionally assigned to clean the toilets in the officers' club, he seizes the opportunity to collect a few old papers on which we all pounce hungrily. Otherwise, we have only rumors, conjecture. No: if we were at war with Algeria, we would have been on maximum alert. So they're preparing us to be sent there. A little war of a few days, enough time to send the troublemakers off to the shooting gallery. A diabolical plan! We'd be legally assassinated. The nation in danger had to be defended and saved, those young people volunteered to stop the Algerian aggressor: the brother whom we'd helped, nourished, protected—and who has forgotten all that.

68

I know, I have too much imagination. The images slip past and repass at high speed. Almost twenty-four per second, the rhythm of a film.

I collect my kit, I hide the papers on which I've written poems, I shave my head and beard. I put on campaign dress. I'm ready. I think of my parents. I mustn't break down. Abdenebi comes to announce that we might go to a military school for training before being sent to the front. After roll call, we climb into the trucks. I notice that neither Akka nor Ababou is there. I see a new arrival, a captain who wears sunglasses even when it's dark. Which it is at five in the morning. The trucks set out. The canvas covers are taut. We see nothing of the landscape, know nothing of where we're going. It's like being a condemned man who loses all notion of time and space. Fear and hunger, shuffled through the jerky cadence of the truck, are sending me to sleep. Actually, I'm just getting drowsy, because I still hear everything. I'm dreaming, filling time with pretty pictures, postcards, clichés of happiness, the little things in life one hopes one day to find. I see sunny prairies with girls rolling hoops, I see a butterfly land on the breast of a girl sunning herself, I see a stream on which glide waterlilies, guided by a frail hand, I see colors, light, joy . . . everything that does not exist in this ordeal savaging our nerves. Now I see nothing: the truck has suddenly stopped. A checkpoint. A sergeant is barking unintelligibly.

"Dere's missink, a bassard, a sumbeechwhat fukinwi me, but it's me, Sergeant Hassan, who'll screw his whore mother . . ."

His anger frightens us. We all pile out. Regroup in sections.

"*Lineupstrate!*" screeches the sergeant.

It's daybreak, we are on top of a mountain. In the distance I can see smoke coming from the roof of a cottage. I imagine that it belongs to a young shepherd and his cousin, now his wife. They live modestly and happily.

"*Balkoum!*"

The sergeant reviews and counts us.

"*Dere's missink, sumbeech,*" he yells again. "Find him, or you'll all pay."

He talks with a superior on a walkie-talkie, sometimes mixing Arabic and Berber with a few mangled French words.

The missing man is Marcel, the only Jew among the ninety-four punished. A decent fellow who'd been arrested while distributing leaflets about Palestine. His father is a militant Communist rather well known in Morocco. The son isn't the kind to disobey, but probably did not wake up this morning, or else he was sick and in the infirmary. That's what the other officer must have told the sergeant, because we caught part of a sentence: "coming along with the support crew." After this unpleasant interlude, we drive on.

The trucks roll slowly, laboring up the steep slopes; the roads are winding, with many sharp turns. Nausea. Feel like throwing up. I hold on. The fellow we call the Weasel has raised the canvas and vomited; it stinks, I hold my nose, and this promiscuity is a problem for me, I'm not made to live with other people. Some men drool in their sleep, others play cards they've made with bits of cardboard, all of them fart, the atmosphere reeks, and I am suffering, yes, I am a weakling, just as Akka told me at the out-set: fragile, civilized, hating being a sardine in a can and there's nothing I can do. I calm down and remember the first lines of "Vowels":

> A black, *E* white, *I* red, *U* green, O blue: vowels,
> One day I will tell where your latent birthplace lies;
>   A, velvety black corset of glittering flies
> Whirling and thrumming 'round odors rank and cruel.

It's precisely those "cruel odors" I'm enduring that bring Rimbaud to mind. Those verses allow me to go on a voyage, break out of this miserable truck. Poetry is my only weapon against these barbarians. The words, the images, the dazzling effects are beyond their control. Rarely has poetry been as necessary to me as during those days. As soon as I can, I jot down lines without thinking about what they mean. I'm obsessed by the myth of Orpheus, and by Spartacus, too. Poetry becomes my ally, my refuge, my bed and my nights. Sometimes I compose in my head until I can find a bit of paper to write my verses down. Before, I used the paper tablecloths in the canteen; now they have plas-tic ones. Once I asked the doctor who wrote me a prescription for a few pages from his pad. Otherwise, Bloom and Dedalus keep me company. Their rambles through a Dublin I've never seen help me to escape, and I wish I could talk to them, leaping through time and space to greet them. I hold the big book close and think, One day I'll be free, and I'll go to Dublin.

My memory has always been a faithful friend, because it

allows me to run away and visit extraordinary places. It is also my solitude. Not that I think myself better than the others, but I am certain that Rimbaud allows me to rise above these moments of loneliness among a humanity with which I share nothing beyond our collective punishment by the king. All this weighs on me more and more and exposes me to danger.

One morning, I lose my temper with a big fellow who's particularly obsequious with the officers. He comes over to needle me simply because I'm from the city of Fez. He's from Marrakesh, and insults me up and down:

"Fezzy, whitey, tricky Jew, plus the Fezzies were old Jewish converts, pesty Fezzy, lousy Fezzy . . ."

No desire to reply. The fist shoots out, the guy falls down, gets up threatening revenge, then the incident is closed. My first and last scuffle. While physical violence doesn't solve a thing, I am surrounded by people who know nothing else. Physical challenges to test our strength and resistance feature heavily in our reprogramming, of course, but there are also sessions of humiliation, like the days we spend supervised by illiterate noncoms who jabber like bandits, and various reminders that our lives depend on a psychopathic warrant officer and an utterly unscrupulous commandant. But the worst of the torments is that we don't know how long we'll be here, or even if we'll ever be released. Even mentioning the subject is painful. One of our number is a chubby guy who plays the simpleton and raves, says he has visions and comes from a family of clairvoyants. One day he falls into a trance, chanting, "No way out, no way out . . ." He claims the camp will be our cemetery. Says he's seen coffins dancing in the courtyard!

■

We are the ninety-four punished, from very different horizons, with diverse habits and traditions, ninety-four young men all arrested the same day with the order "no exceptions," signed by General Oufkir. Fouad, however, a member of the executive committee of UNEM, was quickly freed because his father worked as an informer for the police in Rabat. He is the only one who escaped the punishment. He was, it seems, summoned by an N.C.O. at the Ministry of Defense who scolded him mightily, then pumped him for information about his comrades. Father and son snitches. Another of us saw his detention turn into hospitalization. His name was Zdidane. He was half crazy, became hysterical and uncontrollable when he heard the word *asel*, "honey." Contorting his face, he would scream and lash out at anything within reach. *Asel, masel* (honey-like), *assila* (little honey), all *honey* words drove him mad. He often avoided us, afraid of being provoked by a sadist. One day, a sergeant fed up with his hysteria told a soldier to keep saying the accursed word to him. The poor man fainted, was sent to the infirmary and issued earplugs, but became increasingly irascible and violent. The doctor finally sent him to the military hospital in Rabat, where he finished out his months of captivity.

■

We reach our destination early in the afternoon. It's very cold. I get out of the truck feeling groggy. We're at the top of a mountain, with snow not far away. What is this place called? We line up, our packs on our backs, and wait in front of a big white building. A school or a prison? We're waiting for someone in charge. Suddenly I see the noncoms and lieutenants bustling. Then the commandant of the premises arrives. He's a playboy. Sunglasses, impeccable uniform. "Balkoum!" We're all at attention, stock still.

No speech. He walks up and down the ranks. He's wearing a pungent, spicy scent. That is the first time I smell that perfume. He takes his time, he studies our faces, pouts a bit, then disappears. This is our new commandant.

AHERMOUMOU

We are in Ahermoumou, north of Taza. The building to which we've been transferred is a military training academy for noncoms and officers. "The army is thinking about our future," someone remarks. Yes, a wonderful future. We've left the Stone Age of the camp at El Hajeb for a slightly more modern period. But the treatment is the same. We're supposed to suffer, as Akka has so often told us. A sergeant assigns us to rooms with four beds. The view is superb. A forest, a snowy mountain in the distance, pure air. The fact that we're no longer herded into a single room indicates considerable progress in our story. Dinner is served in a dining hall. Decent but insufficient food. The bread is still the same: as tough as a tire. It must be the trademark of the Royal Army. At the end of the corridor are the showers and toilets. They look clean, and they're nothing like what we went through at El Hajeb.

The next day, the commandant has us assemble in the courtyard. He reviews the ranks again, checks with his baton to see if our heads are well shaved, then slips it into one of his pockets. And suddenly orders us to return immediately to our rooms and sew our pockets shut.

"Here, there's no question of you putting your hands in your pockets, it's strictly forbidden; here no one strolls, saunters, walks, one does everything on the double. Anyone who walks is subject to a week in prison, and our prison is no piece of cake. Moreover, to start things off, tomorrow at five o'clock you will all try it out.

"I continue: here you have reached a superior level. Everything will be superior: the military training, the exercises, the food, and the punishments as well. Don't count on any heat: men afraid of the cold are not men at all. It's freezing and your gray blankets are thin. Reveille is at six; calisthenics at six-fifteen; breakfast at seven-thirty; work begins at eight. Whatever the temperature, you will always assemble in sandals, short pants, and a sweater. Anyone wearing a T-shirt under his sweater will be punished. All cheating will be dealt with severely. Here we are soldiers, not petit bourgeois mama's boys. No weaklings in my school. My orders are to make you flinch, and you will, count on it—and on me, Commandant Hamadi."

Tall, svelte, and even refined, Commandant Hamadi is a born actor. His gestures are studied, his poses and silences worthy of the Actors Studio. Pointedly dramatic and effective communication. Perhaps he's really an actor sent by headquarters to frighten us, make us worry. There's a run-up to each of his appearances. Rumors circulate: the commandant is coming; the commandant is going to make a speech . . . He doesn't show up. Our waiting, perfectly calculated. The perfection of his French raises him above the crowd, a sign of his university education. What is he doing in this place?

■

The next morning at five, without any breakfast, we are indeed all locked up. In a kind of hangar even colder than our rooms. The walls sweat with moisture; no beds, no straw pallets, just icy cement. Clinging together to keep warm? Forbidden. I shiver and silently endure this new torture, going off to one side to lean my head against the wall. Hurting all over, I suddenly think of praying. I don't know why, but reciting a sura of the Qur'an learned by heart when I was a kid helps me endure this little taste of the hell awaiting us. I continue with Rimbaud and feel better. I was a poor student in Qur'anic school, memorizing verses without understanding their meaning, and I would never have thought that one day these verses would come to my rescue in such unusual circumstances. I have a fantastic memory. It's definitely my best friend, even though bad memories sometimes take me by surprise and bring me pain.

We're released from the hangar at around seven that evening. Fourteen hours of arbitrary imprisonment, simply to show us what awaits our disobedience or protests. Commandant Hamadi is well known, it seems, for his exploits in Indochina. He, too, was in the French army in the fifties. He must know Akka. He is also said to be a nephew of General Oufkir. I had not known that gratuitous cruelty was hereditary.

I line up to take my first shower since leaving El Hajeb. The water is cold. We wash ourselves with Tide, a dishwashing detergent powder. I've hated that brand ever since, with its large *T* inscribed within several circles.

Our second dinner is a nice surprise: salad, meat, vegetables. A real meal. Right away, I'm suspicious: if the menu is an improvement, it's because the next correction will be harsher.

I share the room with three other punished men: a pal from Fez, another from Kenitra,[1] and a nice fellow named Salah, quiet, a country man, not a student. He possesses an object I find very interesting: a Philips transistor radio. How was he able to get one and above all, to hide it throughout our time at El Hajeb? He listens to music under the blanket. As for me, I want to hear the news. He lends me the radio in return for my help writing a letter to his family. Since we get along, I ask him why he's among the punished.

He was a shepherd from Beni Mellal, in central Morocco, and was arrested for selling sheep without a permit during Aïd el-Kébir.[2] He is astonished that we others were detained simply for demonstrating. He himself is rather content to be here, saying that it's a lot better than his sheepfold. Some evenings he lends me his radio. I park it against my ear and search out foreign stations for news of the world. I have known nothing for months. I come across a foreign station talking about a young French philosopher arrested in Bolivia because he was a friend of Che Guevara. I learn his name: Régis Debray.[3] He has been in prison for several months. In 1961 I'd followed the ups and downs of the Cuban Revolution during the Bay of Pigs crisis. The fate of this philosopher interests me. I wonder what he was doing in Latin America, why he had felt the need to actually join a revolution so far from his homeland. I figure that Bolivian prisons are as rotten as Ahermoumou's.

I reflect that man is born evil and persists in it because it's the only way he has found to gain power over others. I can see Commandant Hamadi as a Bolivian colonel interrogating Régis Debray. He applies torture even before asking any questions; for him it's a heads-up maneuver, like his imprisonment of us for an entire day. I immediately feel great sympathy for this French philosopher courageous enough to put his ideas and ideals into practice. I think of him and his family and imagine the despair of his loved ones. I hunt for more information on other stations. Before going to sleep, I turn off the radio and stash it under the covers. It's out of the question to get caught with such a thing.

■

In the mornings we attend classes in military matters taught by lieutenants who also speak French correctly. Discipline. Silence in the ranks. We are terrorized for no clear reason. Again I ask myself, Will we stay here forever? For a few months? To be sent somewhere else? To go fight in Algeria? We don't know anything. The lieutenants are as terrified as we are. Commandant Hamadi doesn't joke around with the rules. We all live under his dictatorship, even if we don't often see him.

Our anguish grows. We have passed from elementary brutality to something else again, something disquieting. Among ourselves we call Hamadi the *Aribi*, which means "the hero of the film."

ON SOPHISTICATED BRUTALITY

Collective punishment. A windowpane in the commandant's residence has been broken. Who could have done that?
No one. With his maréchal's baton under his arm, the commandant screams, "I don't even want to know who the guilty person
is; you are supposed to keep watch on one another; this lack of
vigilance shall be punished by exposure for four hours during an
entire week. This is a sample of what I can make you undergo."
Exposure of what? We glance at one another and wonder what
will be exposed and where.

That evening, a sergeant gives us the following orders: tomorrow morning, four o'clock, sweaters, shorts, and sandals, all of us
mustered at attention in the courtyard. Remain standing, mo-
tionless. Anyone who falls will be picked up and punished even
more severely.

We talk in low voices. Warily. In every group, there is always
a spy. We don't say what we think. After all, we're politicals. We
value secrecy and resistance.

It's February; at night the temperature drops below freezing.
The cold drills itself into bodies. Pockets, sewn closed. Hands
freeze. It starts with benumbed ears, the tip of the nose, the fingers. Stay on your feet, rigid, without weakening, resist. No one is

used to this cold. The sergeants who watch us wear warm clothes. They smoke. They drink coffee from a thermos.

What does one think of when the body is icy cold? One doesn't think. Ideas freeze up. No one dreams. We watch minutes and hours go by, very slowly. A first one crumples. The two sergeants pull him up, slap him awake; he straightens up, tries to stay on his feet. Another falls. Same reaction from the guards. I have an idea: what if we all collapse at once? I think better of that right away. The commandant is capable of having us crushed by trucks. After all, who cares about our fate aside from our families, who have no way of knowing what's happening to us? I picture my father going to see one of his Melilla friends, now a general, to beg him to release me. I wasn't imagining things; he did that. I will learn this the day I receive a letter from my father. One has the right to send a single letter and to receive the reply. One letter, no more. Perused, of course, by the commandant's censors. My father writes to me, "I saw your uncle Hadj Muhammad from Melilla; he is tired, no longer goes in to the office." I understand. This uncle had gone to war with Franco against the republicans. They called him the Spaniard. He was the son of a black woman his father had brought back from Senegal, where he had some commercial business. The Spaniard was black as well and had the same name as my father.

My knees hurt. The back of my neck is stiff; my fingers feel dead. I will not fall down. Must not waver, weaken, give in. I will not be slapped. I think of my ex-fiancée. Tears well up, not because of her, but from the cold searing my eyelids. She left me,

deceived and betrayed me. Akka must be behind that punishment as well. It must have been part of his plan. I imagine him
whispering things in my fiancée's ear to aggravate my situation.
This is insane! The stress I'm under is playing tricks on me . . .

I remain on my feet.

■

At eight, we hear a thunderous "Raha!" At ease. We disperse
slowly, as if wounded in war, seeking a place to get warm and
sleep. They serve us bread and coffee. I'm shaking because I feel
my nerves giving way. Fatigue leaves me with no voice, no re-
course.

That day aged us all. The smiling, happy face of my fiancée
is now my constant companion.

In the days that follow, they subject us to the same treatment.
As it happens, the temperature goes up a few degrees. The punishment becomes commonplace. At the end of the week, Commandant Hamadi comes to speak to us about serious events that
might develop at any time. "You must be ready! The enemy gives
no warning, but we—we await them resolutely! We will soon be
visited by a superior officer who will talk to you about what might
happen. To return to the present: those who gave in to the cold
and collapsed will pull fatigue duty for one month. Dismissed!"

What's this business about an enemy? Algeria is called a
"brother country" in the press and the two heads of state exchange congratulatory telegrams on holidays, so why go inventing an enemy? Probably to keep us occupied. You need an objec-

tive in the army. Apparently, ours is to beat Algeria. Absurdity is built into the program.

■

The fasting month of Ramadan is here. How are we going to continue the training, the firearms instruction, the gratuitous punishments? The problem of the moment, however, is Marcel. That confounded Marcel! That funny, unobtrusive fellow who knows hundreds of dirty jokes about Arabs and Jews, who speaks an Arabic dialect with a slight accent like a lisp, that foolhardy Marcel dares to speak up to Commandant Hamadi during an inspection review.

"Commandant, Sir, me I don't do Ramadan, the kitchen has to know about providing my three meals a day."

"Who are you?"

"Soldier Marcel B., serial number 10 362."

"You're a Jew? That's all I needed!"

"It's not my fault, Commandant."

"And now I get insolent backtalk."

"I am a Moroccan citizen and a Jew. We do exist!"

"Yes, I'm aware of that. I don't need a history lesson!"

We are all impressed by Marcel's audacity. No one has ever dared address the commandant that way. Paradoxically, his Jewishness protects him. The commandant happens to know that the king is seriously interested in the welfare of his Jewish citizens. Lowering his voice, Hamadi says,

"You'll eat, but not in front of those who are fasting. You'll go to the kitchen, where you'll have your meal off in a corner. No sense having you seen stuffing yourself . . ."

Marcel thanks him and turns toward us with a triumphant smile.

Once again we're ordered to sew up the pockets of the fatigues just issued to us. Distribution of needles and thread. I sew my pockets. At the last minute I slip in my poems. Good hiding place. I'm getting expert at sewing. I finish the job in a flash. The others bring me their pants; Salah promises me the radio tonight. Another gives me a package of cookies bought from a shepherd who loiters around the shooting range in spite of its barbed-wire enclosure. We give him money and he brings us little things.

The commandant reviews us. Our scalps must be closely shaved. Pockets sewn up; disciplined appearance. He walks along our ranks checking the strength of the pocket closures with his baton; if it gets into the pocket, the wearer gets two brisk blows on the back of the neck. A few blows are delivered. He flips my cap off with the tip of his baton, then glides it across my skull, which was not shaved this morning because of a boil. He stops at that spot, pressing into it until it bleeds. It hurts. I don't flinch. I'm spared the blows on the back of my neck. I stoop to retrieve my cap.

The commandant has summoned us to announce some news; this time it isn't about war: "A superior officer will shortly inspect the school. Pay attention! You must be impeccable: shirts ironed, clean pants, pockets unsealed. Not one word. If he speaks to you, you salute and say, 'Thank you, General.' If anyone dares speak to him about anything at all, he will have me to deal with. Understood? Dismissed."

■

The canteen menu has been improved. While the general's visit is still pending, we know the food won't be too bad. Officers like the troops to be well nourished. Everyone's talking about the visit we're expecting. Some think it's a ruse to test us. One evening, we're allowed to pull out the thread sealing our pockets.

General Driss Ben Omar arrives the next morning. He's popular in the school. A good sort. And for the first time we spend the day with our hands in our pockets. A special pleasure. I even experience a moment of strange nostalgia: the gasoline smell in the wake of the general's convoy sends me voyaging; I inhale it as if it were perfume. To me, gasoline and a rumbling engine mean freedom. I leave the camp, go far away, climb into a limousine and tell the chauffeur, "Onward! Don't stop until we reach the sea." I lower the window and observe the landscape, I look at the people, I guess at their lives. The driver hands me a bottle of mineral water. I drink from a crystal glass. The fresh air is mild. Life is beautiful. The car rolls swiftly along to arrive before sunset. I must see that famous green flash. It is so rare, but today's my lucky day, and besides, the general has gone off in a jeep, leaving his official limousine for me. Comfort is a luxury that does not cross the threshold of reverie.

■

The next day, pockets must be sewn back up. Daily life goes on as before: barely mediocre food; iron discipline; punishment threatened for the slightest mistake or infraction of the rules. One mustn't try to understand.

The winter grows ever harsher. The commandant learns that one of us has a powerful radio and is in contact with abroad. The unfortunate shepherd of Beni Mellal, accused of spying, is condemned to the worst of punishments. I'd already seen it that summer: his entire body will be buried, except for his head, left exposed to the elements. He risks dying of the cold. But my pal the shepherd says nothing. He's a man inured to the severities of the seasons. He allows himself to be led out of the school grounds, escorted by a soldier. The next day, when he is dug up again, he is ashamed: he has pissed and shat himself. That is what enrages him. "The cold is nothing," he tells us, "but soiling yourself without being able to move or wash is worst of all."

As for me, I'm not getting any more news about Régis Debray, who has become a kind of virtual companion. I think about him without knowing his face or his voice. A long-distance complicity unites us, even though his fate is much more dramatic than mine. One of the student organizers whispers to me, "Debray has been condemned to death by Bolivia. He's done for." I feel sad. I imagine a young man, hardly older than we are, a revolutionary, ready to die for his ideas. I think about his parents.

■

Revolt? Absolutely not. A camp ruled by fear functions through time-tested methods. Any rebellion can become a massacre that is then deemed justifiable in defense of the state. Good riddance to those troublemakers, the press won't ever hear about them. Killed for having fomented armed revolt? Legitimate defense! Classic scenario. Perhaps Commandant Hamadi is trying to drive us to such extremities. We sense that he wants blood to flow. Putting down a riot would make him feel useful. The left-wing press knows nothing about this. Some people did learn that young students were sent to the army to do their military service: nothing to get alarmed or indignant about.

▪

Diarrhea. Dysentery caused by our latest meal. Spoiled meat. Some of us have fever, others are vomiting, everyone has colic. We laugh about it. All are equal in the discomforts of a general condition. At least we all remain in the camp the next day. The orderly distributes pills for us to swallow. No one has any appetite anymore, which in itself is a good thing.

▪

In spite of the bromide, two of our companions have gone over the wall during the night to visit the whores. The next morning they're summoned by the commandant, who tells them, "You have already given yourselves your own punishment. All the whores hereabouts are sick; I am not punishing you, I'm waiting until you're no longer able to piss."

The infirmary has been ordered not to take care of them. And indeed, they've both caught a painful case of the clap. It will remain untreated until they can leave the camp, when the malady will have already led to complications. The punishment is a dreadful one.

·

I am summoned by the commandant. I arrive, salute, stand at attention.

"So, you write poems!"

"Yes, commandant."

"I've read them, I didn't understand a thing. Who is this Orpheus?"

"A figure in mythology, a poet and musician . . . It's very ancient history."

"Ah, you write poems about things from another time. Fine, I'm giving them back to you. It's our beloved country you should be writing about and here's an idea for you: why don't you compose a beautiful poem about our magnificent flag for the next Throne Celebration? You see this color? It's the red of our blood, and this green star is our agricultural patrimony, our wealth for which every Moroccan is ready to fight and give his life. Now that's poetry, while you, you hide out in ancient history of no interest."

Stammering, I tell him that poetry is something that can't be controlled. He makes a face, then waves me out.

■

A second window has been broken, this time in the officers' club. The commandant decides on a new kind of collective punishment: each of us must denounce someone; whoever refuses goes to prison for as many days as there are letters in his name. Me, it's ten days. I didn't denounce anyone. Here I am in a cell with two other guys I don't know and who haven't any idea why they are there.

These denunciations produce surprising results. Out of the ninety-three here punished by the king, only twenty snitched on someone. I don't want to judge them; people do what suits them. My father taught me that such things should not be done. He told me about the militants for Moroccan independence who were denounced to the French police during the Protectorate and all tortured or sent into exile, and also about the Jews denounced in France by neighbors, those close to them, people without dignity or morality. He made me understand that within the family, we do not betray others. The commandant is furious. His maneuver has failed. He calls even the twenty informers traitors. After three days, he orders us freed and has us resume training for future maneuvers.

■

It's springtime: the sky is a very soft blue, the air is cool, the mountains white, and the commandant is in a good humor. He has just been made a lieutenant colonel. He announced this to us himself, and to celebrate he has decided to grant us one day's leave. This is the first time that we can leave the school and walk freely in the streets. My parents live just over three hundred miles away. Traveling there to embrace them is impossible. Our leave begins at eight in the morning and ends at midnight. Lateness will incur severe penalties; desertion will be punishable by death. One of the lieutenants has kindly warned us, "Don't try to escape, or your brothers and parents will be the ones to pay a heavy price." He mentions the case of Lahmri, a sergeant who deserted to join a woman with whom he was besotted: caught, he was imprisoned and judged by a special court, as Morocco was then at war with Algeria. He was executed; the press reported it. Executed to set an example. So I settle for a walk through the town of Ahermoumou. Actually, it's a village, where there is nothing. I look for a phone booth. There is none. There is a post office, but it's been closed. I'm told that Hamza the grocer has a phone. I'd pay dearly to hear my mother's voice. Hamza is at the mosque. I wait with a pal of mine. One of the grocer's neighbors advises us to go look for him because he sometimes falls asleep after prayers. And here we are in the mosque, boots in hand, inquiring about Hamza the grocer. And yes, he's quietly napping, leaning against a pillar. I shake him gently. He jerks awake, thinking Satan is nudging him.

"What do you want? Can't a person be left in peace?"

I beg him to go back with us so we can use his phone.

"It doesn't work. I haven't paid the bill, they're such thieves. So I'm through with the phone. Go in peace."

We leave sadly. We eat a tagine of lamb with olives and pre-served lemon. The restaurant isn't very clean but the tagine cooked over coals is good. After eating our fill, we head back. Some women wink at us. My companion is tempted; I hold him back: they are prostitutes who have never seen a doctor. That scares him and we return to the school with relief.

■

The next day, the platoon leaders call the roll and report to the commandant: all present and accounted for!

That day they teach us how to disassemble and reassemble the MAS-36 bolt-action rifle. For the first time I discover how the parts of this weapon fit together. Then we tackle the pistol. I smile, thinking of Humphrey Bogart fiddling with this weapon. After these drills, they have us repeat the assembly and disassembly lessons blindfolded. I flunk. "Ah," the lieutenant says to me, "it's the poet who can't figure it out!" I keep quiet. The others laugh. I'm embarrassed. The commandant is behind this, he wants to make fun of me.

Friday is our day for couscous and the firing range. The guns shoot blanks. Every shot rattles my limbs, especially my shoulder, and leaves me deaf for a few minutes. Rumors are going around: we're being prepared for a lightning strike on the Algerian border. The idea that General Oufkir is trying to eliminate us in a "patri-otic" way keeps running through my head. He's quite capable of it. All last year the French press debated his involvement in the kidnapping and murder of Mehdi Ben Barka. Whipping up a little blitzkrieg with a neighbor and getting us wiped out at the same time . . . I'm suspicious, but those I call the politicals are convinced of it, and one of the leaders of UNEM in particular. He has marshaled his arguments:

"We are political prisoners, even if we don't all have the same status. We represent a risk for those in power. What we have gone through here, what the army has done and is still doing to us, is something the higher-ups want to keep under wraps. The army is not an instrument of repression, and it has a reputation to defend. That's what makes our disappearance a plausible conjecture. They'll turn us into heroes fallen for the fatherland and give us medals when we're dead. The tensions with Algeria are real. Anything can happen."

Suddenly I feel cold, as if an icy wind had just confirmed the hypotheses of this eloquent man. I tell myself that everything is possible, but one can't eliminate ninety-three people in an attack. It's not believable. I keep thinking: possible, impossible, plausible, implausible . . . Anything can happen . . . Why haven't we had any information about how long we'll be held captive? That's understandable: we haven't had a trial, because no government body has officially determined our status. Well, how long does a person's military service last? It depends on the country. Since Morocco had no institution of military service before our arrest, it's impossible to envision any specific release date for us.

■

I'm hungry. We're hungry. The food is decent but insufficient. Besides, we have to carry out all orders on the double. Yesterday some of us repainted the commandant's house. Today, we're out in the sun. We must stand still and remain silent. I guess the big boss must rack his brains every evening to find a new way to mistreat us. I push back against this mistreatment, and I'm proud of that. Hunger gives me migraines. I resist by thinking of a meadow full of flowers and butterflies of every color.

LIBERATION YES, LIBERATION NO

June 5, 1967: War is declared between Israel and the Arab nations. Maximum alert. Assembly at six a.m. The big boss has something to tell us. The heat hasn't yet reached its zenith. We wait. He arrives in battle dress, his baton under his arm. You'd think he was going to film a commercial along the lines of "Join the Army and See the World." He begins:

"The Zionist enemy has struck. Our brothers in Egypt, Syria, and Jordan are fighting valiantly. We must be ready at any moment to go to their aid. As it is, know that we are at war, so remain on the alert! *Attention!* At ease! *Attention!* At ease!"

Marcel is summoned to the lieutenant colonel's office.

Marcel is set free. Orders from Rabat. Now is not the time to risk an incident involving a Jew. Marcel collects his civilian things, puts them in a bag, and bids farewell to us one by one. Some men tell him, "You're lucky," others say, "Hurry back." Still, there are a few who will badmouth him: "Liberated, he'll go fight with his Zionist brothers." Marcel has never felt anything but Moroccan as both Arab and Jew. He belongs to the millions of Jewish families who have always lived side by side with Muslims. But he did tell us one time that someone from the Israeli secret service had come to urge his parents to emigrate to Israel.

His father, from a long line of mattress makers, refused. The agent threatened him with retaliation. The father replied, "I'm fine where I am, I have nothing in common with Poles or Americans simply because we are Jews." The agent had kept at him, but Marcel's father had not given in.

■

After a week, the alert was over. Bitter defeat for the Arabs. No comment within our ranks. Our silence reflects our despair.

We spend the summer on more and more dangerous maneuvers. We are exhausted. We scale a mountain, laden like mules while having to evade enemy fire. Our captain is not playing the game: he protects us, shows us where to hide and rest. He's not happy to be among those chosen to punish us. Later we will learn that he was demoted and posted to the Sahara.

We decide to petition for a little more food. But how can we win our case? One of our politicals asks to see a captain close to the lieutenant colonel: a promise of improvement, but nothing happens. Although we can tell that the lieutenant in charge of our weapons training does not really agree with these words, he drums them into us: "In the army, no protesting, no petitioning, only obedience." So, we're stuck with the skimpy rations. But Halim, one of the politicals, has an idea: ask the shepherd who grazes his flock on the other side of the barbed wire around the shooting range if he's willing to sell us a lamb. To our great surprise, the shepherd accepts. Halim begins to collect the money. Everyone gives what he can. Which adds up to a tidy sum. The shepherd shows us the lamb. But now what do we do? It's simple: he'll take care of everything. He'll cut its throat, prepare it, then deliver it on Friday as roasted méchoui lamb! He takes the money and of course vanishes forever.

The news reaches the ears of the big boss. He laughs, it seems, until he almost chokes. At least this episode preoccupies us for a while; the meals remain the same. Halim asks the big boss if he can go after the shepherd. Not a chance. "That will teach you not to trust just anyone!" Hunger has made us naive.

■

It's July. I've been interned a whole year: not something to celebrate. There's nothing to celebrate—except perhaps that we've survived the whims of psychopaths, had a few close brushes with death, seen men crawl like animals before a sadistic officer, discovered the weak points of a few superiors, and still don't know if one day we will ever leave this prison that will not speak its name. No news from our families. But in his great goodness the boss has allowed us to write to our parents in letters that are read before they are sent. Mine is simple:

> My dear Father, I hope that this letter will find you in good health, will reassure my mother, and bring you both good news. Here everything's fine. We engage in sports, we eat well, and we learn to love and defend our country. Don't worry about anything: everyone takes wonderful care of us. We lack for nothing—except that I miss the sight of your face. May God keep you and grant you long life.

Your son blessed by you.

I know that my father is sharp enough to read between the lines. And anyway, he mustn't be upset.

■

One month later, I receive a letter from my father that I have very carefully preserved, so extraordinary is this document. In refined classical Arabic he informs me of his situation while blessing and addressing me in the language of a great lord forbidden to show emotion:

> In the name of God and His Messenger may Salvation be upon Him.
> Our beloved son, our pride, our grandeur!
> Ever since you left, we know how useful you are to the nation we all of us adore and above all else thanks to our King, may God glorify him and lend him long life and make him triumph over all his adversaries.
> Our beloved son. We are well and we are proud that you have been chosen to serve God, the Nation, and the King! Your mother is well even though she is a little worried from not seeing you more often, but she has a feeling that soon you will come visit her. It must be said that the house is empty without you especially since your brother went to study in France. We are alone with the woman who helps your mother with the housework.

I hope this letter will find you in good and perfect health; we think of you and we await you, dear beloved son.

May God keep you and protect you; may God keep and glorify our King. Long live the King, Long live Morocco!

Your father, humble servant of God.

I read and reread his message. I decode it. My father is aware of the repression and machinations of the military. Reading between the lines: the references to the king are for the censor who will check the letter. I know that my father has never carried in his heart this king whom everyone fears but doesn't really love. I understand that in reality, my mother is ill. I slip the letter under my pillow, thinking that I will see my parents in my dreams.

That night, however, I dream mostly of Ava Gardner. I miss her. Her deep voice, her black and shining eyes, her allure, her insolence, I miss all that. The last time I saw her was in *The Barefoot Contessa*. In fact I miss everything that has anything to do with the movies, which are my absolute passion, and I truly suffer from not going to see them anymore. To think that just a few months before my arrest I saw Sidney Lumet's *The Hill* . . . a film that shows how a sadistic and obsessively strict warrant officer torments military inmates in a prison camp from which not everyone gets out alive. Impressed by the power of this almost documentary-style film that also features exceptionally physical performances by its leads, I thought at the time that what happens in that prison was unreal. I have however been living for a year in a very real remake of that film. Without the camera.

Then, one night, I see my parents dressed in white as though they were returning from Mecca. My mother is crying, my father is gesturing as if to calm me. They speak but I cannot hear their voices. The more I approach them, the farther away they are. White is an evil omen, it's the color of mourning. Later I will learn that Nadia, my eighteen-year-old niece, died asphyxiated by gas fumes while taking her bath.

■

More than a year without music. Does anyone care? Around me, no one complains about it. I mention it but find no sympathetic and complicit ear. I call upon my memory and by concentrating can hear the first flights of some John Coltrane. Then I review the songs of Léo Ferré and Jean Ferrat. I make a huge effort to recover the rhythms, chords, rhymes, and words. I remember the poems of Aragon interpreted by my two favorite singers.[1] I go astray; I am not concentrating enough; the songs withdraw into a complete silence: they are no longer anything but memories of memories. I try to conjure up movies again. I concentrate and I say "Lights, camera, action!" . . . It's Marcel Carné's *Children of Paradise*.[2] The images stream by but not the sound. It's strange. Suddenly I recognize the inimitable voice of the great Jean-Louis Barrault. Then nothing more. The film goes away. The screen is all white, and I fall asleep.

∎

Rumors. Hamadi is leaving. Hamadi has been promoted; he will no longer oversee those punished by the king, a degrading task. Hamadi is ill; the king supposedly sent him on the pilgrimage to Mecca. Hamadi is getting married. Hamadi has been made a military advisor at the Moroccan embassy in Washington. Hamadi is in prison. In short, hearsay abounds and changes every day. What is certain is that Hamadi has left Ahermoumou. No one has seen him. There is no light in his office or residence. He has left. His absence is evident. The soldiers no longer move on the double. A sign of laxity. The terror is gone. Hamadi has been summoned by Oufkir: promotion or punishment?

∎

His replacements arrived while we slept, in the middle of the night: Commandant Ababou and his assistant, Chief Warrant Officer Akka.

Assembly at seven. Ababou, followed by Akka, reviews the ranks. They are both in a bad mood. Not one smile, not one word. They're tense. Promotion or punishment? Both, apparently. They're moving from the camp at El Hajeb to the military training academy . . . but they're in charge of those punished by the king. Not really an advancement. We'll find out right away. Ababou addresses us:

"Here we all are again. This time the correction must be impeccable. No weakness, no sloppiness: I will be ruthless. Your training is not over. Commandant Hamadi—excuse me, Lieutenant Colonel Hamadi—has been appointed to other functions. I noticed that there has been some slackening off in the ranks. This is unacceptable. So everyone on the double, we're going to run, you will run in place for an hour without stopping. I leave you with Chief Warrant Officer Akka. Attennnntion! At ease and one two, one two, faster, really step on it!"

Ababou disappears. Akka yells and strikes one or another of us with his baton now and then. A gratuitous blow just to remind us that he likes to lash out abusively.

"As my superior Commandant Ababou says," he shouts, 'No pity for weaklings!' You're all weaklings, wet rags!"

We begin to miss Hamadi. For Ababou seems possessed by rancor, resentment, and even hatred. He isn't pleased to be here, and vents all his nervous tension on us. He's compelled to do this. Strange: he didn't invoke the name of the king. He must simply have forgotten. We run, we run, Akka behind us with a baton. Hearts pounding. This isn't the moment to break down, to fall. We must hang on. The smokers are the ones who collapse first, which allows Akka to kick them. They get up and fall again. He insults them, calls them faggots, pathetic wimps . . .

Tough day. After the run, we go off for improvised maneuvers, which are really just to keep us busy and make us sweat. We're back in the old camp routines. Akka is furious, and in front of everyone he humiliates a staff sergeant who has disrespectfully forgotten to salute him. Shortly thereafter, a lieutenant gathers us together and advises us to say nothing: "You haven't seen a thing, you have nothing to report."

After Ababou returned, reveille was moved forward an hour. At five we are on a war footing. A permanent tension maintained by Akka. "Just what will he be able to do with us?" wonders the unlucky sergeant. Well, here's one idea: surprise one of our own sections outside our cohort and attack it.

"I've learned that Section D has gone off into the country-side for a picnic. Can you imagine? A picnic! So our comman-dant has decided that you will go flush them out while they're enjoying themselves. That'll teach them to let their guard down. Distribution of weapons, backpack, helmet, departure in four-teen minutes."

We leave the school heading on the double for a plain on the other side of the mountain. It's hot. No rest. We run, led by Akka. He is indomitable. As we advance, he gives a speech intended to energize us.

"The country is in danger, His Majesty is in danger, we have to intervene, to quickly defeat the plot. So while they're having fun eating fancy dishes and enjoying nice drinks, we'll surprise them: don't hesitate, shoot them, we're at war, we've no choice, come on, one two, one two . . ."

I ask myself, Is he crazy? I say nothing and I run. My rifle is heavy, my backpack is heavy, the heat adds weight to everything. How is it possible that a section of the school could dare to attack the king? It's insane. Yes, Akka really is crazy and dangerous. I remain alert. When we reach the place of the supposed picnic, no one is there. It's a joke. Akka is furious. He was misinformed. He tries to save face.

"It was simply a way of motivating you to reach a goal. I hope you will always be ready to save our country. Repeat after me," he shouts: "Allah, Al Watan, Al Malik!" God, the Nation, the King.

We automatically repeat that motto written everywhere on the walls of the academy.

A quarter hour to rest; then back to the academy. Along the way I try to figure out where Akka gets his authority: although only a warrant officer, he has more power than a captain. Perhaps he owes his life or his career to Ababou, who controls him and at the same time trusts him completely. There must be a pact between them, something signed in blood.

■

The first days of October 1967. The mountain is beautiful, the trees stand fast, unshakable. The sky is pale blue. I hear the diesel engine of a country bus. I love this noise that reminds me of trips between Tangier and Casablanca, between Fez and Tangier. Once more I catch myself breathing in this smell of low-grade fuel that intoxicates me beyond all logic. I think of where I've been during the beginning of the university school year. I imagine our metaphysics professor, M. Chenu, explaining texts by Nietzsche; I remember his passion for Kant and his lyrical effusions when expounding on Heidegger. All that is far away. I remember things, but cannot even begin to formulate a philosophical argument. This environment distances us from the world, from intelligence, subtlety, it makes us strangers to the realm of spirituality, knowledge, and the exchange of ideas. Here, no thoughts, no ideas, only more and more stupid orders with an edge of cruelty along the way. Poets and philosophers here are undesirables: unthinkable, excluded. We are reduced to our basest instincts, our bestial, animal, unconscious elements. They've done everything to strip us of what engages us to think, to reflect. At night I struggle with myself, trying not to become like my three roommates, who resemble military robots. They accept everything without flinching, as if their brains had been left in the luggage locker of some derelict station. They are here, content with what they have become, passing the time joking around and preparing to be good little soldiers under the commandant's orders.

There's no chance of deceiving that man. I am quite alone. I have no one to confide in, to talk to, so I talk to myself, and I'm afraid I'll go mad in the end. Rachid, a former mathematics teacher, has lost his mind. They shut him up in a room all alone and he beats his head against the walls. He's a good man, quite thin, frail and discreet. I don't know how things suddenly turned serious. One day he did not get out of bed, refused to eat. "He wants to quit work and go on hunger strike," shouted Akka, "but here there's no such thing. I'm going to put him through the wringer until he forgets even his name . . ." That's exactly what happened: Rachid no longer knows his name or where he is. He'll look at us haggardly, then lie down on the floor, curl up tightly, and lie silent and still.

I think about my ex-fiancée, who must be blissfully in love with a young man who's free and well off. I'm not angry at her, but it hurts when her image invades my thoughts. Wait: yes, I am angry at her, I detest her, I hate her. A beautiful woman, rebellious, insolent, a free spirit, as my older brother says. Would I try to see her again if I'm set free one day? I don't know. No one has ever seen a love affair rekindled thanks to explanations! It's past history. Should be forgotten, completely.

I'm told that Rachid was sent home to his family. Will he regain his reason there? Probably. Some claim he faked madness to escape that prison. Everything is possible: we're in a world where nothing functions normally. Soldiers are anesthetized, their officers are half demented. They, too, are punished.

Akka is nervous; he comes and goes with his hands clasped behind his back. Ababou is not pleased. The story of the surprise attack did not go over well with the commandant. We get scraps of information from the staff of the canteen. Their ears stretch everywhere.

We're given to understand that something is going on: a different camp, even more arduous maneuvers, or several days' leave, or the commandant is getting married, or Akka is sending his wife back up country . . . A strange atmosphere. The sky is gray. This autumn seems like an early winter. It's cold. A rabid dog bit a sergeant, who was sent to the hospital in Rabat. Akka set out with a few soldiers to hunt dogs and he killed a few. It seems that prostitutes visited some young officers, which was discovered when a lieutenant developed virulent blennorrhagia. He went off to Rabat as well. Ababou is angry. Headquarters is not communicating. He feels isolated. And now he invites the main politicals over for dinner. There are three, all members of leftist parties. They are serious, take themselves seriously, and think they can teach the commandant something. They are naive. They inform us afterward that Ababou is a leftist: it seems he confessed to them how distasteful he found his duties as a prison warden. They believed him. He was testing them. They failed to realize that he is shrewder, more prudent than they are. I can see that Ababou is a complicated man of whom one should be wary, but I have no say in the matter. I'm only a grassroots activist, a student who believes in justice and the law. It appears that in his home the commandant has a picture of Oufkir, autographed like the photos of movie stars. Oufkir! That's dreadful! They say his wife is quite lovely and that he shares her with the king. They say so many things . . . Who could verify the truth of everything people say? I don't see myself gravely asking General Oufkir if his wife really is the mistress of Hassan II. Solitude makes us think about shameful things. What do I have to do with the wife of this general reputed to be a killer? Nothing. Better just drop it. But if I were a superman, I would park him on a chair and grill him about his hand in the disappearance of Mehdi Ben Barka.

Beginning in mid-November, the rumors about our release become insistent. The doctor who arrives every Friday has the best information. Dr. Noury comes from a poor family in the north of Morocco. Only the army offered him any financial aid for his medical studies, so he became an army doctor. He told one of the politicals that some higher-ups at headquarters took a dim view of our "punishment," that two officers had even argued bitterly about it, and that the Palace had gotten wind of the business. At the same time, our release poses a problem: now that we have suffered so much mistreatment, it would be hard to keep us completely quiet about how His Majesty's army deals with the young people of our nation. Commandant Ababou has supposedly received very specific orders to prepare for our release from prison: better food, no more frequent and dangerous maneuvers, and we'll be allowed to go on leave. In short, they want to treat us better to make us forget what we have endured.

An ambitious program. Akka distributes packs of playing cards and cartons of Troupe cigarettes, has our bedding changed, and asks us not to shave our heads anymore. His honeyed words are completely false and hypocritical.

These new measures provoke worried discussions among us. The politicals, who are often summoned by Ababou, report that he says the whole situation was forced on him by certain important noncommissioned officers and that, anyway, he has taught us things that we'll find useful one day. He believes in the importance of "military service" and insists that it wasn't punishment, just military training a bit tougher than usual, and that when he himself was in boot camp, he had it worse than we do . . .

Abruptly, at the beginning of December, a new reversal of our situation. The decks of cards are collected, our food is again crummy and insufficient, Akka puts us back on the double, and his tone turns hard and threatening.

■

It's snowing on Ahermoumou. We're very cold. The officers' quarters are heated. A guy from Sefrou confirms it: he spent the night with Lieutenant L., who likes boys. Our fellow has managed to worm some things out of him while sleeping with him. Our release seems to be imminent. Certain bigwig officers at headquarters don't like the Royal Army being used for extortion and settling political scores. The order has supposedly been given to release everyone. But the commandant doesn't see things that way. He's dragging things out and prolonging our sufferings through below-freezing temperatures. Every day, one of us is summoned to receive a morale lecture and a warning that if he talks when he gets out, the commandant will bring him back to endure terrible tortures. Then he has him sign a letter affirming that he has spent his military service under good conditions, and thanking the Royal Army for its warm welcome and kind treatment . . .

We organize a secret meeting to refuse to sign that piece of junk. We don't invite the fellow from Sefrou, the lieutenant's little friend. Impossible to take the risk of pillow talk ruining our plan. A watchword makes the rounds: sign nothing.

We carry the day. No more signatures. The commandant gives up. Orders have arrived from Rabat to speed up our release. The commandant drags things out as much as he can, releasing four to six of us a week. The threats are all made viva voce. Before leaving the school, a medical checkup. We are not ill, but our general condition is not good. Our morale in particular has suffered, although the idea of regaining our freedom does give us some hope. We're afraid of traps. No confidence in these dirty brutes. We don't know how Ababou and Akka choose whom to release. No logic, no criteria. We wait. I realize that our trials have not created any bonds, any friendships: we put up with one another, but don't talk about getting together again in civilian life. That's normal, it seems. See one another again? Why? To remember the long days of sadness, exhaustion, and misery? We're still anxious among ourselves for no precise reason. I retreat into silence, do not participate in animated discussions—there's no point to them. I'm afraid they will keep us here; anything is possible. At night I have more and more explicit nightmares: imprisoned for life, fear, cries, chaos, madness . . . I'm surrounded by rats; I hate those creatures, I'm allergic even to the sight of them. Rats and moles, they're at home in this prison—I'm an intruder who disturbs them. Some bite me, others lick my face, I scream for help, no one comes, I've no more voice, no sound comes out of my throat, the rats dance and laugh, whirling around me, their new prey, I feel tired, I'm done for, I let myself be devoured, and I die in my sleep. My shrieks awaken my three companions. Each has had this kind of dream. Usually we don't talk about them, in an effort, perhaps, to ward off their malignant power. Even bone weary, we don't sleep well. We're eaten away inside by the turn our fortunes seem to be taking. How will this "military service" imprisonment end? Getting out, yes, but when, and in what state? I have evil premonitions. Maybe the truck taking us back to the city will lose its brakes and wind up in a ravine. An accident. They'll tell our parents, "It's God's will!" I try to go back to sleep and forget the maybe-out-of-control truck. I find rest by focusing my thoughts only on my grandmother Lalla Malika, whom I dearly love.

                      ■

In the morning, I look at myself in the mirror: I'm thinner, pale, bleary-eyed. Need air, need to take a hot bath, need to drink some good coffee and go for a walk. I feel sick, have a nervous fit; someone mentions epilepsy; I'm taken to the infirmary. The doctor isn't there yet. I'm given hot coffee and stretched out under a blanket smelling of naphthalene. My heart is pounding. "You have to be sent home," the doctor says, "it's the only remedy." For once, I believe it: I know that I'll be leaving this accursed place, I know that if I don't get out I will make the walls pull back of their own accord. I smell the odor of those little white mothballs that repel fleas and mites. It's the last stink I will carry away from this prison.

I am strong, I'm no longer afraid, I know that we have triumphed over those who tried to bring us to heel, I leave with the sure knowledge that they are pathetic wretches, the garbage of this army that fosters a deep racism between those of the South, the Amazigh, and those of the North, the Rif; between the people of the cities and those of the countryside, between those who can read and write and those who jabber in anger. I take off my army clothes. They hand me back a bag containing my white shirt and my gray trousers. They're dirty. So what. After nineteen months, they're too big for me. I put them on. I've lost a good twenty-two pounds. I wait for my papers. In Administration I see Captain Allioua, the one who tore up my medical exemption certificate. He hasn't changed: a fake smile, dead eyes, the indifference of those from the North. He wants to say a few words; I don't listen. A pile of red tape. Stamps, signatures, remarks . . . When we part he stares at me with a finger to his lips: Not one peep! Yes, silence, we won't denounce you, you bunch of bastards, no, we'll paint an idyllic picture of our stay, young men will rush to join an army that punishes instead of educating, that terrorizes instead of unveiling new horizons, an army where they recruit psychopaths instead of sending them to consult Dr. Benaboud, an excellent psychiatrist, a humanist, and a philosopher who lives in Salé, just outside Rabat.

The day after the coffee in the infirmary, someone motions for me to head for the exit. Akka is there, whistling under his breath. Zaki and Larbi, two guys from Tangier, have been selected along with me. We're still afraid. We don't dare believe it. I glance one last time at Akka. We walk faster. As we cross the threshold, Akka says to us, with a strange smile, "See you soon!"

We don't answer. But we think, yes, that's it, soon, you bastard, we'll meet again in a court of law with honest judges, people who will apply the law with perfect integrity, people horrified by this system that tortures, disappears opponents, or parks them in a camp run by heartless and perverse executioners. Zaki leans toward me and asks, lowering his voice as if we were still in the camp and being spied on, "You think the king knows about what they did to us?"

I reply in a normal voice, while he tries frantically to hush me.

"The king? He doesn't give a fuck about us, he doesn't even know we exist and that we're suffering."

We wait for a taxi. We count the money: not enough to get to Tangier, more than eight hours' drive from the camp. The car is an old yellow Mercedes that must have been a taxi during the Second World War. The driver looks at us aghast, as if faced with space aliens.

"Where did you come from?"

"From the army," replies Larbi. Zaki pipes up: "We were on vacation at Akka's place."

We negotiate the price. We pay him an advance and promise him the rest when we get home.

We set out. Zaki in front, Larbi and I in the back. The driver smokes. It bothers me but I don't dare say so. I watch the landscape stream by and reflect that nothing has changed. Larbi, always carefree, sleeps deeply and snores. Zaki chats with the driver so he'll stay awake. Me, I daydream without managing to drift off to sleep, oppressed by incoherent images. I'm not thinking of anything. I let myself be lulled as if after great exhaustion.

At Fez, we stop for some coffee. It's Zaki who pays. Finally, some *real* coffee, I'd forgotten the taste of it. The driver eats a big sandwich and drinks a Coke. I walk a few steps to make sure that I'm really free, released. I raise my arms, I jump, I do anything at all, I shout, I run, and come back to the taxi. People must think I'm loony. And I was lucky not to wind up that way. This time I go to sleep in the taxi, and wake up in Larache, a large harbor town. It's nighttime. No one in the streets. I sense the presence of the sea. I breathe deeply and tell myself, That's it, the house isn't far now, another two or three hours on the road.

ON THE OUTSIDE

January 28, 1968: I arrive home in the evening. My parents have not been informed of my release. I'm standing at their front door. The light is still on. The driver is waiting. I ring. My father asks, "Who's there?" and opens the door. I fall into his arms; we both weep. My mother runs up and lets out ululations that wake up the neighborhood. My father embraces the driver and invites him in. I give him two hundred dirhams. It's one in the morning. Rahma, the household help, wakes up: "I'll fix you something to eat." I'm not hungry, or, rather, I don't know what I want. I'm here and I'm not here. A strange feeling. The world and I are reeling, and I don't know where to touch down. My mother exclaims over how thin I've gotten; I confess that it doesn't bother me. I swallow two mouthfuls of chicken with olives and feel fatigue overpowering me. I nod off on the cushions in the dining room. My father, as he did when I was a child, carries me to my room, draws the covers over me, and I hear him praying. My mother is worried, doesn't know what to do, and wiping at her tears says, "The bastards, they've destroyed my son."

But it's impossible to sleep, really; the soft bed doesn't suit me. I feel a kind of malaise at this comfort, a rejection. I lie down on the thin carpet. The hard floor makes me think of the stones that used to jab at my spine. I roll over, roll back. I've returned from my ordeal with a new friend: insomnia. I suffer from it still. I think I've tried everything to recover peaceful and deep sleep. But there's no help for it, sleeping has become a rare, even impossible thing. And now I don't eat, I just swallow. My stomach hurts. I don't even enjoy the fine dishes my mother makes. After all, I can't really ask her to cook with camel fat and let the bread get stale for days. Reentry is a whole new struggle requiring time and patience.

After bolting some food, I finally take a bath, relax, put on clean clothes. I'm recovering myself little by little with an eye, perhaps, to telling my story. Rahma whispers to me that my ex-fiancée has left the village, gone off with a Christian. It doesn't matter. I no longer think about her. Need to remake myself. The whole family arrives. My big brother, who had gone with me that day, is here; the brother studying in Grenoble phones me and admits that he had been afraid for me. My sister has come as well, along with her husband, their eldest daughter, my aunt, my two uncles, their children, some neighbors, friends of my father, and my rebellious cousin, the one who went to prison for saying that in this country, corruption begins at the top. Three years in prison for insulting His Majesty. My cousin had not mentioned him but was condemned anyway.

It's a celebration. I'm worn out, a bit sad. I go up to the terrace and look at the sea. Beautiful weather. The strait is calm. One can see the shores of Spain. I think of the militants imprisoned by Franco. Despotism and repression flourish there, too. I stay a good while in the sunshine, imagining life on the other side of the water. For the first time, I feel I have been set free. I no longer belong to them. But am I free? I will not even be able to tell the story of our suffering. I remember Debray, the French philosopher, and wonder if he is still imprisoned in Bolivia. Two years later, I will learn of his release. I feel as if with my liberation, all prisoners of conscience ought to be set free. I see a fisherman's boat, hear the sound of the engine and I wish I could be on that boat. My mother calls me: lunch is ready. She got up very early this morning to prepare everything that I love.

I'm greeted with questions, hugs, cries of joy. My aunt, the one who's afraid of nothing, says bluntly, "Now, we'll have to find him a wife, poor fellow, he must be famished, we'll marry him off to a girl of good family, a girl who'll be honored to love him . . ." Everyone laughs. Yes to needing a woman, but not for getting married. I call a friend who was with me at the university, who tells me about the courses I must still complete. I'm missing one certificate for my philosophy degree. It's now February. I have time to present my dissertation in June.

My parents tell me how shocked they were by my ex-fiancée's behavior. They were ashamed. I reassure them: It's nothing, I say, I'm no longer fond of her. It's difficult to discuss this painful subject with them. It hurts me, and I try not to show it. What's the use of explaining to them that I love that girl of scandalous beauty?

My mother has her diabetes to take care of. My father coughs, even though he stopped smoking. My big brother talks to me about Nadia, the daughter he lost, and the immense sorrow that has fallen on the family. Rahma brings me up to date on all that has happened since I left, and mixes everything together: "The grocer died suddenly, no one misses him, he was mean and dirty, they say he was bitten by a rat while he was sleeping in his shop; it's his son who's taken over, he's nice and gives everyone credit; the neighbor's son is in prison, he sold kif to a flic, he's a jerk; your aunt dreams of you marrying her daughter, you know, the skinny one who can't find a husband; one of your girl cousins almost died because of gas, yes, she was saved just in time; the king made a speech in which he condemns girls who wear very short skirts; your big sister went off to Mecca for the second time and came back cured of all her ills . . . Enough, now rest!"

∎

A need for movies, a visceral need to see images streaming past, to be in a darkened theater, waiting for the film to begin, to sit through the poorly made commercials, to listen to the weekly news bulletins dealing almost exclusively with the royal court. When the king doesn't figure in a news story, it's in black and white. As soon as it's about the royal family, everything is filmed in bright colors. I put up with these boring newsreels and think about Ava Gardner and Richard Burton because I'm here for John Huston's *Night of the Iguana*. The film is slow in starting.

The audience grows impatient. Someone informs us all that the bicycle messenger bringing the reels has had an accident and is in the hospital; as for the film, it's at the police station. People shout, they protest. Another fellow gets up on the stage. "You're in luck!" he exclaims. "We have a great film as a replacement: a magnificent love story that even won the Palme d'Or at Cannes." Silence in the theater. Then the man announces . . . *A Man and a Woman*. Consternation. We're used to seeing only American films in this theater, and now they're foisting off on us a French film by Claude Lelouch. Disappointed but resigned—I still have the reflex of military submission—I do not protest. I would never have waited in line to see one of his films. It begins. A lemonade vendor goes by shouting, "Coca Judor, Coca Judor!" Spectators rise and leave the theater. Me, I stay until the end even though I hate every shot. Lelouch is a good cameraman but a pathetic film director. He has nothing to say and says it pretentiously. That throbbing, monotonous music finally puts me off for good.

As I'd hoped, seeing images flow by has done me good, however. The next day, Ava Gardner explodes from the screen. She has a few bruises on her arms. The messenger's bicycle accident has almost disfigured her. I catch up by watching the movie twice. John Huston is incredible.

On the other hand, ever since that day I've felt a deep-seated aversion for Claude Lelouch. Unjustly. I know he has his fans. My friend Amidou, the Moroccan actor who began his career with him, has told me a great deal about him. Amidou hasn't changed my mind, but when you do love something, you don't understand the why of that, either. Let's say that I will always resent Lelouch's having stepped in for Huston that day . . .

＊

I leave for Rabat to continue my philosophy studies. Along with poetry, philosophy was my pillar and my crutch. The source of all knowledge, fueling my conviction that through its study we consolidate our dignity as human beings and citizens. Rabat has not changed. It's a city where everything stands still. At the Faculty of Letters, however, I can't find any of my former comrades. Some are teaching, others have gone abroad to write theses. But M. Chenu is still there: friendly, likeable, you can see his red cheeks are veined with violet, it's the alcohol. He gives me a list of works to read and when we part, says, "It was hard, wasn't it?"

"Yes."

On my way to the Cité Universitaire, I pass a military barracks. I look at the soldier on guard duty. I can hear shouts of "Balkoum!" And "Raha!" Attention . . . At ease . . . I smile. There are no lodgings available at the Cité anymore, and I'm sent off to Father Gilles, who runs La Source, where he rents rooms to students. There I meet a Frenchman, a painter; desperate, he borrows money from me, then disappears. Father Gilles tells me he's an unfortunate soul, nice but rather disoriented. I'm to be in charge of the film club once a week. I show *The Leopard*, followed by a lively debate about Visconti's classicism. I'm happy because I feel thousands of miles from the camp. I'm coming back to life, I do useless things, find it fun to go treasure hunting in flea markets and then buy roasted peanuts I eat with a glass of sweet mint tea. I grow lazy. I'm strolling idly and I love that. But as night approaches I feel increasingly afraid and then panicky. I am alone; I reason with myself, out loud, to dissipate this tension. I recognize the anguish: the nature of this state is that it gives no warning. It arrives, that's all. You don't know why or how. With my hands I push away the approaching night. I look at the sky and call for light. Some stars streak away and others keep shining.

The camp and its ghosts obsess me. I keep seeing the poor soldier who must have died buried alive. I see again the hard face, the pitiless gaze of Chief Warrant Officer Akka. All that builds up in my head and strengthens the migraine. I'm still keeping track of days and nights; 564 days with nights that are not really nights, some of them are so short. We were time itself, and we had to walk along to accompany it until the sky changed its light. I am freed but not free. The camp weighs heavily. I carry it on my shoulders. My back is strained and weary. The camp haunts me, with its dreadful winters and suffocating summers. I have to get out of there, get rid of it. Insomnia digs a furrow through my aching body. This all takes place in silence. Above all, don't speak of it, don't complain: that would only aggravate the situation. And then there is an odor difficult to describe, to define. It invades me from time to time. The odor of El Hajeb, something humid and greasy, viscous. I hold my nose and wait for it to fade away. My mother has given what were my clothes to the neighbors' sons. I've gotten so thin that nothing fits me.

■

James Joyce's novel, dragged along with me everywhere, is now dirty, with that indescribable odor of captivity. When I open it, I can't manage to get past one or two pages: I don't read it, I remember. And those memories smell bad. Forgive me, Monsieur Joyce, but your masterpiece has been stained by ordeals of which you have no idea. It has become mixed up with something brutal. It has been soiled by a sad and nauseating context, but its presence has helped me, given me hope and ideas. Your audacity of creation has marked me, made me dream of one day attaining something that would approach that boldness, a promise of freedom from the pettiness and pain of the world.

■

I visit Abdel, one of my former professors. I give him the few pages written during captivity. Still drawing on his extinguished pipe, he reads and murmurs, "It's good, it's strong . . ." He offers to send the pages to a friend, the poet Abdellatif Laâbi, who has just launched a poetry review, *Souffles* (Breaths).[1]

Time has changed color and intensity. I tackle several difficult texts and work without respite; some of them find a special resonance within me. I read Nietzsche. *Thus Spake Zarathustra* becomes my bedside book. I read it as a novel. I take notes. Then I tackle *The Gay Science*. Neither deaf nor deafened, I am happy to be so comforted in my still stammering ideas. I love when the philosopher evokes the "religion of pity" and the "religion of comfort."

In any case there is only one thing for us to do: admit death and not neglect the felicities of life, by striving never to shame another human being, and never to humiliate intelligence and our presence in the world. One must build up one's self enough to avoid going astray amid the noise and disturbance of the times. The image of the eternal hourglass of existence fascinates me and explains my resistance to sleep. Shat upon by Nietzsche's "dirty birds of our time," I keep a lively mind ready to learn, because as Nietzsche says, thus "we become limpid once more." And Zarathustra says, "Thoughts that come on doves' feet guide the world." It's at this moment that I discover Spinoza and adopt one of his ideas: "Everything that is tends to persevere in its being." That is my motto, a thought that came to me on doves' feet. Even if we modify certain parameters, not only does no one change, but the whole world persists in its certainties even unto death.

I could have come out of the camp changed, hardened, an adept at force and even violence, but I left as I had arrived, full of illusions and tenderness for humanity. I know that I am mistaken. But without that ordeal and those injustices I would never have written anything.

■

In June 1968, I receive my degree in philosophy. In July, I'm given my posting: teaching in Tétouan, a city known for being very conservative and rather unwelcoming.

Souffles publishes my poems. I'm beside myself with joy. Readers write to me. I'm in heaven. My students talk to me about my poetry. Then someone asks me, "So, when's the next poem?" I don't say anything and think, I have to keep going . . . In Tétouan as in the rest of Morocco no one has heard anything about the military camp. When I'm asked about my absence, I reply, "I was on vacation in Ahermoumou." People repeat the name, garbling it, not knowing even whether it's a village or a country.

Three years later, at the end of May, I receive a summons, signed by Commandant Ababou, to appear on August 1 at the camp at El Hajeb. I call my former comrades: they have received one too. I have no desire to go through that again. I think about running away, going into exile. My parents agree with me. I am a philosophy teacher at Lycée Mohammed V in Casablanca. The school year has been quite short. Given the strikes, the arrests of students, repression of all kinds has already driven me to prepare to leave for France. No scholarship, no stipend. The ministry won't budge. I'm on contract, and if I want to leave I must repay the state for the advance I received while earning my philosophy degree. I couldn't care less. I have to leave. Abdel advises me to take a year's sabbatical without pay. At the ministry I see an old gentleman who gives me to understand that he knows what trials I've been through. "I will make an exception and grant you a leave of absence, renewable for three years, contingent upon justification of your studies. Otherwise, you will be required to reimburse the Moroccan state for their cost." As a teacher I earn 905 dirhams a month. Just enough for food and lodging. Impossible to save any money.

■

It's definite. With my last month's salary I buy a plane ticket to Paris. Departure planned for mid-July 1971. Because of the events that follow, my departure will be delayed by two months. Muhammad Ouassini, who is also leaving, has offered to put me up for a few days in the home of an aunt who lives in Charenton, just southeast of Paris.

■

On June 5, I am in Fez with two of the punished men for the medical exam required by our call-up. I'd best follow the rules even if I've already decided not to return to the camp. I don't talk about it. Toward noon, we're about to enter the café-brasserie La Renaissance, right in the center of the modern part of Fez. And voilà: we find ourselves face to face with Commandant Ababou. Shock. Followed by a reflex: we stand at attention! Ababou, who is dressed casually in sports clothes, reminds us that we're not in the army. My pal Larbi, the optimist, the man who's always smiling, asks him point-blank: "Commandant, we're in Fez for the medical exam for the call-up this coming August 1. Why this recall, Commandant?"

I can still hear and will never forget what Ababou says next: "I've got a surprise for you, a big surprise." Larbi, worried and excited, wants to know what it is. "You'll see," replies the commandant, "a surprise, I tell you." Zaki doesn't laugh. He's convinced the army wants to get us back to enlist us for real. I try to distance myself from all of it. In any case, I reflect, on August 1, I'll be in France.

Commandant Ababou gives us a friendly pat on the shoulder before going off, repeating, "Surprise, surprise . . ." We're left stunned, troubled, with fear in our bellies. We just happen to know what this commandant, a man utterly devoid of humor, can do. His surprise can only be a new ordeal, a fresh catastrophe. He is not the kind to joke around, especially with former "punished" men.

We take a table and order brochettes. Larbi laughs loudly, nervously. "He's nuts, that commandant," he says. "He thinks we're going to obey him like we used to!" Zaki, still pessimistic, replies, "We've received an official document, a summons from the army; if we don't show up we're considered deserters and then—the punishments are ferocious. Me? I don't feel like laughing about it. They're poisoning our lives." I jump in: "You remember the guy who deserted? He was buried alive . . ."

Larbi wonders what the surprise could be. War with Algeria? Shit, if that's it, it'll be terrible. No desire to shoot at Algerians, they're brothers, cousins, they just barely got through an appalling war with France . . . Shit and double shit. The Sand War is within living memory. Perhaps generals of the Royal Army want to replay that conflict and break up a still-fragile Algeria.

We've lost our appetites. The return train leaves at around five o'clock. We try to distract ourselves; Larbi attempts to pick up two tourists, Scandinavian girls. "We're going to rub up against democracy! Fucking a girl born with democracy in her blood, that has to be better than good!" I've no desire to hit on girls. I'm anxious about the "surprise."

Once back in Tangier, Larbi leaves with the two girls and tells me to join him later. He lives quite close to my parents' house, in a tumble-down palace. We spend the night there making love to Swedish democracy. I admit that in the morning I feel light, happy, changed. The girls smoked, first. Personally, I hate that. We exchange addresses, and I go home. I don't tell my parents about the "surprise." The next day, the girls take the boat to Algeciras.

THE SURPRISE

July 10, 1971, 2:08 p.m. One thousand four hundred officer cadets, traveling in twenty-five trucks, surround the summer residence of King Hassan II, a palace by the beach, about twelve miles from Rabat. Lieutenant Colonel M'Hamed Ababou enters the Skhirat Palace by the north gate. His older brother, Muhammad, by the south gate. It is the king's birthday. He is forty-two years old. He has organized a garden party to which he invited his friends, some diplomats, politicians, artists, military men. Casual dress. Light music. The king likes to go against protocol now and then. The sky is a special blue. It's a hot day. The order is given to kill everyone. Machine-gun massacre. Blood in the pool, on the sand, on the buffet tables, everywhere. The king hides in a bathroom.

It's a holiday. We set out in the morning with some friends for Rmilat, a few miles from Tangier, for a picnic. Girls and boys. Larbi is there. He's funny, he makes us laugh. We eat sandwiches from Abdelmalek's, they're famous. We drink Cokes. Everything goes well. The weather is beautiful. No east wind. Tangier is at its best. Larbi jokes about our supposed return to the army. The girls say, "We'll follow you." We giggle, we kiss. We're happy. Only Zaki is in a foul mood. "He's bringing bad luck," Larbi tells me;

"you'll see, we'll wind up in that shithole army!" Zaki is sensitive about his shortness and kinky hair. He compensates by being really smart and a bit derisive. He's gloomy, as usual. He's the opposite of Larbi. Me, I'm somewhere in between.

Toward three-thirty, we decide to leave. Coming up from the bay we reach the esplanade where there is a café popular with families. It's empty. That's strange. One of the girls wants to go to the bathroom. As soon as she gets inside the café she runs back out: "Come quick, come in, there's a guy on TV who's gone crazy!" We rush in and see a well-known journalist, Bendadouch, looking quite somber, reading a communiqué:

> The army has just seized power . . . The monarchical system of government has been swept away . . . The people's army has taken control . . . Vigilance, vigilance . . . Any other communiqués will be reported to you . . . The people have been set free, the corrupt monarchy no longer exists . . . It's the revolution of the people and the army! Remain vigilant . . .

Military music punctuates this declaration. One of us says, "That's it, it's the revolution; quick, let's go to the National Trade Union Center—the workers must be out in the streets . . ." There's no one left in the café; outside, not one bus or taxi. We begin to run to get back into the city. We hitchhike. A Renault 4 stops: it's our former history teacher, a Frenchman. We pile into the car, and he's the one who tells us what's going on: "Some soldiers have launched a coup d'état; a certain Aba -bu or -bou is their leader. They fired on everyone, the king must have been killed, seems there are hundreds dead . . . This looks bad. It's the end of Morocco!" We can hardly believe it. We look at one another with a sinking sensation. Someone turns on the radio: military music, the reading of the army communiqué. Ababou! Larbi bursts out laughing. It's nervous laughter. Zaki protests and calls for silence. He says it's a historic moment and we might all be shot!

■

Ababou! Of course! The "surprise"! The big surprise! So that was it! Zaki is dying of fright. He's pale. Silent. Larbi's not laughing anymore. He's petrified, too. We all are. My throat's dry. I panic and already see myself a soldier on the Algerian front. My imagination is jumping around and I've lost all control. Need to pee. Everyone needs to pee. The teacher stops the car and there we all are, relieving ourselves. Some have stomachaches. We've stopped talking. We're anxious to get back.

At the workers center, there's no one. The streets are deserted. We scatter and everyone heads for home. My parents are dreadfully worried. Especially my father, who knows what soldiers can do. So do I, with good reason. I go to my room without managing to calm down. I straighten things up a bit. I turn on the radio; the national station isn't broadcasting, so I hunt for a foreign one. I find Radio France. I wait for the hourly news bulletin. A special correspondent reports:

"Rabat is in the hands of the rebels, I hear gunfire around the national radio building where the rebels are proclaiming the republic; there are many dead among the king's guests, impossible to estimate how many. The French ambassador managed to escape; the ambassador from Belgium is dead. Impossible to know the situation of the king. A communiqué states that he has abdicated. The officer cadets came down from the military academy at Ahermoumou, a village in the northeast of the country; their leader is a lieutenant colonel named M'Hamed Ababou, seconded by a henchman, a certain Akka, followed by young officers including the brother of Ababou. I've been handed some names: Captain Chellat, Captain Manouzi, Adjutant Mzirek. Some generals appear to be accomplices of Ababou: there's been mention of General Medbouh, very close to the king, the director of the Royal Household, today the shadow leader of the rebel soldiers. As for General Oufkir, they say he has taken charge of the loyal army and is now searching for Ababou and his men. In Arabic, Medbouh means Cutthroat, a fearsome name . . ."

And all these names echo in my head, because I can put a face to each of them. They are the officers who punished us. The very ones who put us through nineteen months of martyrdom. Those officers have become killers. In the case of Akka, I'm not surprised. They're out of their minds to want to overthrow the king through violence. They aren't going to survive this, at least that's what I hope and tell myself. If their coup ever succeeds, I know what they will do with this country: it will be an appalling and pitiless dictatorship. Ababou, impulsive, angry, violent, cannot be a democrat. They speak of justice and democracy, but these are people who fear neither God nor man. I know them. I say this to myself over and over: "I know them, I know them."

My brother calls from France. He says the French army would be ready to intervene to save the king. To save Morocco from possible takeover by violent and uneducated soldiers thirsting for power. It's utter confusion.

I become as worried as the monarchy: I've just realized that our summons of August 1 has a direct connection with the coup d'état. Ababou must have been thinking of enrolling us in his adventure. The worst part—retrospective fear—is that he might have launched this coup while we were in his hands. Ninety-four leftist students, there's a good alibi for a future dictator. We had a narrow escape. It's even a miracle. Nothing was stopping Ababou from keeping us and dragging us into a tragic undertaking, and I wonder why he didn't. He had complete power over us, for we had no way to disobey him. Besides, he wouldn't have told us anything about his intentions. As he did with the young officer cadets, it was later reported, he would have drugged us and told us that the king was in danger, so we were going to save him!

I can see Akka's hard face again, his shaved skull. I see the determined stride of Lieutenant, now Captain Manouzi; I imagine Captain Chellat wiping out the king's guests. I hear the name of Boulhim, of Allioua, the one who tore up my medical certificate; they say those two are looking for Ababou to arrest him and bring him to the king. General Medbouh is arrested and killed by Akka for having wanted to spare the lives of the king and his family.

Late that night, ears glued to my transistor, I hear the announcer for Radio France interrupt a theatrical program to announce: "The king is alive; he has just issued the following statement . . ." The king speaks of divine intervention, of friendship betrayed, of God's blessing, says he would rather be the victim of a friendship than betray a friend . . . He is reassuring, speaks in impeccable French. We learn that a hundred of his guests have been slain. That his brother Moulay Abdallah is slightly wounded, that Crown Prince Sidi Mohammed, eight years old, is safe and unharmed.

The radio station has been retaken from the rebel soldiers. People say that the Egyptian singer Abdel Halim Hafez, who was there recording a song, refused to read the rebels' communiqué. It seems they threatened him, but he said he was a foreign artist and would not interfere in the politics of a friendly country. It was the blind Moroccan composer Abdessalam Amer who was forced to announce the fall of the monarchical regime. They read it to him; he learned it by heart and recited it.

I feel better. Even though I wasn't involved in the bloodshed at the king's garden party. In fact, amazingly, I have just escaped disaster by the skin of my teeth. Had Ababou triumphed, I wouldn't have given much for our lives — we, the men punished by Hassan II. Ababou would have forced us to reenlist and shot anyone daring to resist. Ababou was like that. It was even because of his reputation as an uncompromising soldier that Oufkir had entrusted him with the task of reforming the students opposed to the regime. Mission accomplished. Still, the commandant hadn't managed to get everything he wanted: to make us accomplices, rebels, martyrs.

What followed was only to be expected: live on television, the execution of the generals implicated in the coup d'état. Before being shot, they are humiliated, degraded, chained, and dumped into a truck. The others, the officer cadets, are all arrested. Ababou was shot by General Bouhali at the entrance of headquarters in Rabat. Akka ran away. Caught in the outskirts of Kenitra, he is mowed down like a dog. The monarchy settles its scores. And I, I still shiver at the idea that we might have been dragged into this reckless adventure by that power-hungry psychopath.

My mother prepares an enormous couscous for the poor. "God is with us," she tells me. God or chance, God or destiny.

▪

For having demonstrated calmly, peacefully, for a little democracy, I was punished. For months, I was nothing more than a serial number: 10 366. One day, when I had given up hope, I found freedom again. I was finally able, as I had dreamed of doing, to love, travel, and write many books. But to compose *The Punishment*, to dare to return to this story and find the words for it, has in the end taken me almost fifty years.

Off to El Hajeb

1. Kif is a substance, usually cannabis, smoked in Algeria and Morocco to produce drowsiness or intoxication.

2. A hammam is a public bathhouse long popular in much of the Islamic world, using water and steam, often with massage and scrubbing by attendants.

3. Moulay (Lord) or Lalla (Lady) are Berber titles of respect for family members or nobility, and Moulay Idriss Zerhoun is a holy town near Mount Zerhoun in northern Morocco, founded in 788 by Idriss I, who took materials for its construction from the nearby ruins of the Roman city of Volubilis. A great-great-great-grandson of the Prophet, Idriss I was the patriarch of the Idrisid Dynasty (788–974), considered the creators of the first Moroccan state.

4. A haik is a large rectangle of cotton or woolen cloth, usually white, worn wrapped around the head and body as a loose outer garment by North African men and women.

5. In the foothills of the Middle Atlas Mountains, El Hajeb is largely inhabited by descendants of Berber tribes once known as fierce warriors. The Berbers are the indigenous peoples of North Africa west of the Nile Valley, where their culture probably dates back more than four thousand years. Some scholars maintain that El Hejab was first settled during the Almohad Caliphate of the twelfth century and later destroyed during shifting tribal conflicts, but the present El Hajeb was itself an important military base in modern times, and the ruins of the original kasbah (the fortified core

area of a walled town or building) may still be seen today. Built by Sultan Moulay Hassan I (1836–1894) to keep at bay the local tribal powers, El-Hajeb protected Meknès, one of the four imperial cities of Morocco along with Fez, Marrakesh, and Rabat, all capitals in revolving succession during the long centuries of various dynasties, caliphates, and sultanates while Morocco evolved into a unified nation and, at the end of the French protectorate (1912–1956), achieved independence. Hassan I's greatest success was to strengthen his regime through reform and to increase tribal loyalties to the *makhzen*, an ancient notion in Morocco that roughly embodies the feudal state Morocco represented before the protectorate, when *bilād al-Makhzen*, "country of the *makhzen*," meant land under central government authority, and *bilād as-Siba*, "country of dissidence," was the tribal flux of areas outside the governing institution of a unified state.

Last Moments of Freedom

1. Mehdi Ben Barka, a gifted mathematician and former math tutor of the then Prince Moulay Hassan, was one of the founders of UNEM, formed in Rabat after independence in 1956. His radical politics and economic development programs made him a leader of the Moroccan opposition to the regimes of Mohammed V (1909–1961) and his son Hassan II (1929–1999). After criticizing Hassan II for waging a border war against Algeria in 1963, Ben Barka fled into exile as an apostle of revolution among developing nations. Condemned to death in absentia, he survived several assassination attempts, but after months of secret surveillance, he was lured to Paris, where on October 29, 1965, he was disappeared in an uncanny foreshadowing of the savage murder of the Saudi journalist Jamal Khashoggi, a prominent dissident and critic of the Saudi leadership, who was murdered in Istanbul inside the Saudi consulate by agents of the Saudi government, who dismembered and destroyed his body.

French trial records and the reports of investigative journalists determined that French and Moroccan intelligence agents kidnapped Ben

Barka at noon in front of the famed Brasserie Lipp and took him to a house outside Paris, where he was tortured to death. His body was never found, and in 1967 Interior Minister (General) Mohamad Oufkir was convicted of his murder in absentia. Mossad and the CIA are rumored to have been involved as well.

2. Directed by Sidney Lumet, *The Hill* is a 1965 film about a British army stockade in the Libyan desert during World War II. Much scenery is chewed in this melodramatic but undeniably grueling version of the classic mix of helpless prisoners, sadistic officers, and brutal punishment. Centered on the power struggles among the captives, their torturers, and the decent officers who try to keep the camp on an even keel, things come to a frightening pitch when five new arrivals are forced to repeatedly carry heavy burdens up and down a manmade hill in the center of the camp, and one of them dies.

Akka

1. Also called Tamazight or Amazigh, the Berber languages are closely related dialects spoken throughout Northern Africa and, as of the early 1950s, in Berber immigrant communities in western Europe. The Berbers predated the Arab conquest of the Maghreb (*Al-Maġrib*, "the West," in Arabic), and they and "Arabized" Berbers are now the heart of the native populations there. Many Berbers also speak Arabic, variants of Maghrebi Arabic, and French in the postcolonial regions of the Maghreb, so the linguistic inheritance of Morocco is a complicated one. Berbers often feel that they and their languages are the victims of discrimination, because although French was long officially recognized in Morocco, for example, Berber did not become a constitutionally official language there until 2011. This language barrier can be a lifelong problem for Berbers, who tend to live in rural areas and have historically been left out of the political process, so they are often considered "backward" by Arabs.

Mohammed V Hospital

1. *Chikhate* is a Moroccan term for musicians, singers, and dancers, often in a traveling troupe of entertainers. Formerly, female entertainers were often also prostitutes, a tradition that modern Morocco has tried to suppress. Contemporary videos online show images of raucous celebrations with impressive displays of plump but fully clothed belly dancing.

A *cheikha* is also a female Moroccan singer, an artist in the honored Bedouin tradition of *Al-aïta*, poetry sung to music: *aïta* means "cry" or "lament," and is one of the many traditional musical forms that Sultan Hassan I revived at the end of the nineteenth century. His patronage was bestowed on many revered Chikhates, but in the unrest that followed his death in 1894, the singer most remembered is the legendary Hadda Al Ghaîtia, known as Kharboucha, a member of the Oulad Zayd tribe. In that time of bilād al-Makhzen and bilād as-Siba, she survived the massacre of her village by a treacherous rival tribe and attacked its powerful caïd through shocking songs of denunciation and defiance unheard of in the Bedouin culture.

2. When *Aden Arabie* (1931), a collection of essays by the French writer and philosopher Paul Nizan, was republished in 1960 with an introduction by Jean-Paul Sartre, this opening became an important catchphrase for the student protestors of May 1968 in Paris. Their demonstrations against military and bureaucratic elites spread quickly throughout France, becoming part of a worldwide escalation of conflict between revolutionary movements and political repression.

3. *Méchoui*, a North African dish, is traditionally prepared by roasting a whole lamb or sheep on a spit or in a pit in the ground, so the meat is tender enough to pull off the bones and serve and eat with the bare right hand. The entire animal is consumed, and the host will select choice pieces to offer to guests, with the organs — including the eyes — saved for guests of honor.

An Evening chez Ababou

1. The history of early Islamic Morocco (c. 700–c. 1060) already has ancient Carthage at its back, starts off with the Muslim conquest, encompasses various revolts, kingdoms, dynasties, and polities, spends about five hundred years with the Almoravid, Almohad, Marinid, and Wattasid dynasties, then another hundred years with the Saadi dynasty, and hits the ground running for the Alaouite dynasty in 1666, which, remarkably, is still enthroned today. The Alaouite family claim descent from the Prophet Muhammad and probably arrived in Morocco at the end of the thirteenth century, a pedigree that carries great weight on its home ground. So the two portraits on Commandant Ababou's wall come with some baggage.

Morocco's contacts with Europe and the United States were not always happy ones, as the country was still struggling to unite itself into a centralized, modern state with secure borders, and in the later 1800s, Muhammad IV and Hassan I saw the French gain ever more influence in their affairs, until Morocco was forced to recognize a French protectorate (1912–1956). This was a bitter time, with unrest and Berber revolts against both foreign occupiers and central authorities. The resentment of the populace under the humiliating jurisdiction of French courts helped spark an independence movement and the foundation in 1944 of the Istiqlal, or Independence Party, a conservative and monarchist party supported by Mohammed V. Deposed and exiled, he returned in 1955 just before independence to rule as king until his death in 1961. Mohammed V is remembered with some affection by his subjects and with gratitude by the Moroccan Jews who sheltered beneath his protection from the Nazis and Vichy French.

Hassan II (r. 1961–1999) is another story. The eldest son of Mohammed V, he accompanied him into exile and back, served him as a political advisor, was at his side in the negotiations for independence in 1956, and was his army chief of staff for Morocco's first Royal Armed Forces, leading troops fighting rebels in the Rif mountains. Superbly prepared for the job, he became king in 1971 at the death of his father. His life was a long and busy one, on the national and international levels. He was intelligent, capable, wily, charming, ferocious, loyal and treacherous by turn, and Morocco is the only Arab monarchy remaining in Africa, a constitutional monarchy that Hassan II ruled with the classic iron hand. And from roughly the 1960s through the 1980s, that iron hand put Morocco through what are known as the "years of lead": appalling and often deadly state violence against peaceful protesters, strikers, dissidents, and activists calling for democracy, thousands of whom were jailed, tortured, exiled, killed, or disappeared. When Tahar Ben Jelloun opens his chapter "Last Moments of Freedom" with "A leaden sun. It's part of the drama I'm caught up in," he is waving from the edge of the pit of political oppression into which he will now vanish, and from which many did not return.

Ahermoumou

1. In 1912–1913, the Moroccan resident-general under the French protectorate, Hubert Lyautey, established a French fort, town, and port at Kenitra. During World War II, Americans captured the air base at Port Lyautey, which the navy operated until control reverted to France in 1947. The United States shared the base with Morocco throughout the Cold War, leaving in 1991.

2. Aïd el-Kébir celebrates Abraham's willingness to sacrifice his son at the command of God, who provided a ram in the boy's stead. Each household slaughtering an animal traditionally keeps a third of the meat, gives a third to relatives, and the rest to the poor.

3. Born in 1940, Jules Régis Debray is a French philosophy teacher, journalist, and writer best known for his radical theories and his adventures in South America. While teaching in Cuba at the University of Havana, Debray was recruited by Castro in 1967 as an emissary to his former second-in-command, Che Guevara, who was in Bolivia on an ill-fated military campaign to foment a Marxist revolution. Debray was arrested after leaving Guevara's camp, however, and Bolivian forces soon captured

Guevara. Convicted of being a guerrilla, Debray was sentenced in November 1967 to thirty years in prison, but he was released in 1970 after appeals were made by religious, political, and cultural figures such as General de Gaulle, Françoise Sagan, Noam Chomsky, Hannah Arendt, Jean-Paul Sartre, and even (unofficially) the pope. Debray holed up in Chile, interviewed Salvador Allende for his book *The Chilean Revolution* (1972), and returned to France, where he continues the life of a dedicated intellectual theorist and gadfly.

Liberation Yes, Liberation No

1. Léo Ferré (1916–1993) was a poet, composer, singer, and pianist, who as a child was sent away for eight traumatic years to a strict Catholic boarding school in Italy, from which he emerged as a self-proclaimed anarchist, but one who had discovered the blessed art of music. After further studies and the Occupation, he went to Paris, where he slowly clawed his way up from Bohemian poverty to success, eventually releasing forty albums and many hit singles, some of which are classics. He became the epitome of a *chanteur engagé*: a politically committed artist.

So was Jean Ferrat (1930–2010), a French singer-songwriter and poet, a *chanteur de texte* presenting songs of literary quality, in particular the poetry of Louis Aragon. A lifelong Communist, Ferrat never joined the Party and even criticized its failings, but his left-wing sympathies informed his work, endearing him to the public but irritating the authorities. As a teenager, he had taken refuge with Communists when the Vichy police shipped his father to Auschwitz, where he died; years later, Ferrat's deeply moving song about the Nazi camps, "Nuit et Brouillard" (Night and Fog), was banned by the French state-controlled media.

A member of the Académie Goncourt, Louis Aragon (1897–1982) was a French journalist, poet, and novelist, one of the great names in French literature. Active in the cultural movements of dadaism and surrealism, he broke with them in 1931 to support the French Communist Party and the literary doctrines of socialist realism. After 1940 his poetry and novels took a more traditional turn, and by the end of the 1950s many of his poems had reached a wide popular audience when set to music and sung by stars including Yves Montand, Georges Brassens, Ferré, Ferrat, and Catherine Sauvage.

2. This is the Wikipedia entry of November 15, 2019, and it is perfect: "*Les Enfants du Paradis*, released as *Children of Paradise* in North America, is a 1945 French epic romantic drama film directed by Marcel Carné. It was made during the German occupation of France during World War II. Set against the Parisian theatre scene of the 1820s and 1830s, it tells the story of a beautiful courtesan, Garance, and the four men who love her in their own ways: a mime artist, an actor, a criminal and an aristocrat." The movie is three hours long, and always wonderful.

On the Outside

1. Born in Fez in 1942, Abdellatif Laâbi is a poet who in 1966, with other poets, founded the influential French and Arabic literary magazine *Souffles*, which quickly became a forum for creative people of all kinds and cultures throughout the Maghreb and the developing world. *Souffles* was published in Rabat until 1972, when the repressive regime of Hassan II subjected Laâbi to torture and sentenced him to prison for "crimes of opinion" (1972–1981). In 1985 he went into exile in Paris, where he still lives and writes as a prize-winning poet, novelist, playwright, and translator.

Mysteries remain about the failed Skhirat coup d'état in 1971 and the next attack on Hassan II, on August 16, 1972: fighter jets from Kenitra Air Base strafed his plane but did not kill the king. His revenge was swift. Mohamad Oufkir—the monarch's closest confidant, whom he had made defense minister after the general put down the first coup—died that very night. Like the plotters of Skhirat, Oufkir had supposedly become disgusted with the corruption of the king's regime, although some feel he secretly helped the previous conspirators, if only to clear his own way to more power. The Palace claimed he had killed himself out of remorse for his treason that day.

This was disputed by the Oufkir family; the eldest daughter, Malika, eighteen at the time, had seen her father's bullet-riddled body. Oufkir's widow, Fatéma Oufkir, and her six children—the youngest a toddler—were put under house arrest and soon shunted into increasingly harsh confinements in the southern desert of Morocco, ending with a secret prison in Bir-Jdid, a deathtrap intended to kill them slowly. In her book *Stolen Lives*, Malika Oufkir describes the malnourished family's misery without books or other simple comforts, medical care, or even basic necessities. Plagued by brutal guards, illness, grueling heat and cold in damp cells infested with scorpions and filthy vermin, kept often in darkness, isolated from the outside world, and for long years at the end even separated from one another, "We were entering the realm of insanity."

Between 1978 and 1986, Malika and her three sisters shared a cell, with her mother and two brothers in adjacent cells, the oldest boy all by himself. For eight years, schooling and consoling them as best she could, Malika tried to teach her sisters about the life they were missing. In 1986 the family was moved to a single cell, where one night they all tried to kill themselves by opening veins with scraps of metal. In 1987, crazed with despair, Malika, one sister, and the two boys tunneled their way out with their fingers, a spoon, a knife handle and a sardine-can lid, only to wander in terror of recapture in a world they could hardly recognize. Malika finally obtained the phone number of Radio France Internationale, and the world learned of their appalling plight. Forced to release them after their fifteen years of anguish, the vengeful king held them under house arrest until 1991, then kept them in Morocco for another five years until Malika's sister Maria escaped to Spain in 1996 to sound a second alarm, and the world was again outraged. The whole family was eventually allowed to leave the country.

That happy ending was not granted to those punished for the 1971 assault on the king at Skhirat. General Medbouh and Lieutenant Colonel Ababou, the chief instigators, had trucked in well-armed officer cadets from the Royal Academy at Ahermoumou and launched them at the birthday reception. The cadets were supposedly told either that they were simply on a military maneuver or that the crowd of people there intended to assassinate the king, and some witnesses said the cadets went berserk at the sight of so much luxury. (An official Palace communiqué later claimed the cadets had been drugged beforehand.) Troops loyal to the king arrived, turning the attack into a gun battle lasting several hours. The king hid in the bathroom and was unharmed; about two hundred cadets were killed by friendly fire, and around a hundred were shot by loyal soldiers, who rounded up some nine hundred others. Although the principals of the attack were immediately shot, the king was persuaded to pardon the remaining cadets, although some were sentenced to serve various terms in the Kenitra military prison, and at least fifty-eight wound up in Tazmamart.

This secret subterranean prison, off in the Atlas Mountains of southeastern Morocco, was built after the Skhirat attack to punish dissidents, in particular would-be assassins of the king. It was more a pitch-black tomb than a prison: of the fifty-eight cadets, twenty-eight survived, and only because the world finally found out about them. Some told their stories: in his *Tazmamart: Cellule 10*, Ahmed Marzouki describes how, believing himself on a military exercise, he found a massacre at Skhirat, where he never fired a shot and tried to stop the carnage. His reward: a five-year sentence. Two years later, the king's vengeance sent him to rot forever at Tazmamart in a cramped individual cell, where men's vermin-infested bodies became "one immense wound" and their ever-growing hair, beards, and nails changed them into "phantoms drifting in prehistoric caves."

The memories of another survivor provided Tahar Ben Jelloun with the material for his award-winning *This Blinding Absence of Light*. In a cell less than ten feet long, about half as wide, and impossible to stand up in, there was "a hole for pissing and crapping. A hole not even four inches wide. The hole was a part of our bodies. We had to forget our existence fast, stop smelling the shit and urine, stop smelling anything at all." To remember was fatal: "Anyone who summoned up his past would promptly die," coming alive only to realize that they were all already "in our graves." The prison had been designed *specifically* to torture inmates to death infinitely slowly: engineers and doctors had studied "all the possibilities for prolonged suffering."

Once a day, the inmates were given just enough to keep the body alive while the mind died: a bowl of slop they compared to camel piss, and bread hard and tasteless as a rock. The concrete sleeping platform sucked out the body's last heat in the bitter cold, when limbs and joints would stiffen so "we could not even rub our hands together or pass them over our faces. We were as rigid as corpses." There were no doctors; the skittering of scorpions in the dark could be deadly, and tuberculosis was the prevalent disease. One inmate with a wasting sickness was even supposed to have been taken to a military hospital on the way to Skhirat, but the commander forgot about him. At death, "The folded knees had worn a hole in his rib cage, and the ribs had worked their way into the joints. Impossible to unbend the arms or legs. His body was a ball, all bony. It probably weighed less than ninety pounds." But the most horrific torment of all was the permanent darkness, a scourge that dissolved memory, logic, will, madness itself—even the soul: "Night was no longer night, since there were no more days, no more stars, no more moon, no more sky. We were the night."

Although human rights organizations had begun investigations during the 1980s, and rumors about Tazmamart served to terrorize the Moroccan opposition, the regime consistently denied its existence until pressure from these groups and some foreign governments finally forced King Hassan II to release all surviving prisoners and close Tazmamart in 1991.

The 1990s in Morocco saw a slow and grudging relaxation of oppressive government controls in the human rights and political arenas. King Hassan II died in 1999, and the accession to the throne of his son, Mohammed VI, has seen further reforms. Morocco is still the only Arab constitutional monarchy in Africa.

TAHAR BEN JELLOUN, born in Fez, Morocco, in 1947, is an author, poet, and now painter who learned French at school in Tangier and studied philosophy at the Mohammed V University in Rabat. In 1966, he helped found the magazine *Souffles*, which championed a new linguistic aesthetics promoting contacts between the French and Arab literary worlds. His first collection of poems, in French, was published in 1971. Later that year, for political and professional reasons, he moved to Paris to study psychology, in which he earned a doctorate. He soon began writing articles for *Le Monde*, and, already a prolific writer, he published a dozen literary works before his novel *The Sand Child* (1985) brought him wide acclaim. The sequel, *The Sacred Night* (1987), won him the Goncourt Prize, and *This Blinding Absence of Light* brought him the 2004 International IMPAC Dublin Literary Award. Elected to the Académie Goncourt in 2008, Morocco's most famous literary son and a stalwart of French literature, Tahar Ben Jelloun has published more than sixty books. Showered with honors and distinctions, he is the most translated francophone author in the world.

LINDA COVERDALE has a Ph.D. in French Studies from Johns Hopkins University, a B.F.A. from the Parsons School of Design, is a Chevalier de l'Ordre des Arts et des Lettres, and has translated over eighty books, by authors including Roland Barthes, Emmanuel Carrère, Patrick Chamoiseau, Annie Ernaux, Marie Darrieussecq, Jean Echenoz, Marguerite Duras, and Georges Simenon. She has translated Tahar Ben Jelloun's *Leaving Tangier*, *A Palace in the Old Village*, *The Punishment*, and *This Blinding Absence of Light*, which won the 2004 International IMPAC Dublin Literary Award for both author and translator. She has also won the 2006 Scott Moncrief Prize, the 1997, 2008, and 2019 French-American Foundation Translation Prize, and the 2019 Best Translated Book Award. She lived in France as a child, grew up on Long Island, and now lives in Brooklyn.